Broadcasting Christmas Cheer

Camille Cabrera

Dedicated:

To the hopeful creative. Keep creating
a kinder, better world.

Introduction

Madison Crawford can't believe she landed her dream job as a broadcast reporter after graduate school. An unexpectedly lucky break. Eager to prove her merit, she started working and never looked back. Six months later, Lakewood still doesn't feel like home. Rocko, her pet hamster, seems to be her closest companion and often comes with her on multi-day excursions. While filming a restaurant segment, Rocko breaks free and scuttles into the upcoming hotspot's packed dining room. Madison attempts to make amends as the health department lays down a harsh punishment against the small town establishment.

It's out of the fire and into the frying pan as one accident ignites the next. A question dances around the back of Madison's mind. Are the local spots all experiencing simultaneous health code blues, or is a more sinister plan cooking behind the scenes?

With the town's Christmas fundraiser only a few weeks away, Madison leaps into the mystery that might make or break more than just her career.

Chapter 1

People bustled out of the shop almost as quickly as they came in. The crowd moved around the bakery in droves while Madison sat in silence. Watching.

"Aren't you happy you moved to Lakewood? You'll never find another town with tastier strudel."

Angie proudly held up her half-chomped pastry and clinked it against the side of Madison's steaming cup of hot chocolate.

Madison's smile didn't fully reach her coffee-colored eyes as she gave her new friend a half-hearted smile.

"Yes, I never had a snack like this in New York. To be fair, I rarely went out for a bite to eat in the city. Who knew that I needed to move all the way to Colorado to find such an awesome family-run place?"

"Sweetie's Bakery is the gift that keeps on giving. I hope the new bakery down the street knows what they've gotten into. This town has a competitive food scene that runs several generations deep. Sweetie's Bakery is a town favorite. Anyways, don't worry, Madison. It's normal to feel homesick after such a large move; especially so close to the holidays. Besides, you've barely been here a month. It's going to take a little time for you to feel settled!"

Madison winced, "I moved here six months ago."

"Already?"

Angie swallowed her last bite. Her pearly award-winning smile glimmered in the cheerful sunlight as she added, "Time flies when most of your life is work. It's hard to find the time when you're a news reporter in a small town, but you'll get used to it. If you think about it, the holidays are chaotic wherever you move. Let's see how you feel by the start of the new year."

The bakery's location was originally an old home. The 1800s home was recently converted into one of the most popular shops in town. Apparently, the bakery has outgrown its previous location. Madison's brown orbs took in the dining area. The owner preserved the structure's old-world charm and embraced the massive wooden pillars. She saw the vision. A vision that made it difficult to find a better place to grab a snack. Madison loved that the bakery offered free pastries at the end of the day. Who knew giving away day-old pastries could be such a genius way to avoid food waste?

Madison hummed in the back of her throat. If the new bakery was even half as delicious as this one, she was in for a treat. Literally.

Still, she didn't like feeling left out. Angie seemed so settled into the motions of her daily life. Madison wondered if she could have something like that in the future. A future that seemed to be slipping through Madison's fingers by the minute. After six months, all Madison had to show for her move across the country was a winding list of text messages between her and her not-so-new boss.

"What's the name of the new bakery?"

Angie covered her mouth as she spoke over a pile of pastry, "I think it starts with the letter A."

"Angel?"

"Something like that."

The kind words bolstered Madison's courage as she leaned back against the wooden chair. Patrons of the tiny bakery bustled near the front of the store. Madison had to hand it to them, Sweetie's Bakery definitely had a reputation. Upbeat music charged the air as customers came and went through the front door. Luckily, the people behind the counter seemed to be pros at getting people where they needed to go.

Madison soaked in the bakery's atmosphere as Angie reached for her second pastry. Large green and red ornaments hung from cheerful garlands wrapped around the exposed wooden rafters while twinkle lights cast the room in a soft glow.

Angie pulled out her phone between bites and snapped a photo of the elaborate decorations. Madison shot her friend a curious glance.

"What? You don't like taking photos?"

Madison shrugged, "I haven't really felt the need to take any pictures. I like to take photos whenever something feels important."

"How many pictures have you taken since moving here? Before you say anything, work-related photos don't count."

Madison balked, "We don't know if I was about to include work photos. Let me see."

She made a big show of opening her phone and searching through her photos, only to be sadly disappointed. Three images. Two of those photos she'd snapped and sent to her parents to show off her cozy new place. She'd been so proud of her new home just inside of the forest. The owners had even included the furniture. The third photo in her camera roll? Oh, that didn't count. She'd taken a photo of the promising new skate park for an upcoming assignment.

The Lakewood community sure loved to skate.

"I see your point, Angie."

Angie hummed in acknowledgment and swallowed another generous gulp of her drink. Madison enjoyed the rare occasion when her mind could move away from work-isolated sentiments. Maybe she did need to make more of an effort to fit in. The realization popped her previous excitement like a bright balloon brushing against a sewing needle.

Madison found it impossible to feel down for long when surrounded by such an upbeat atmosphere. She looked around the room and realized Angie was the only familiar face.

"You're right, I did jump in. But sometimes I worry that I jumped headfirst. Working as a news reporter right out of school is amazing. To be fair, I did take my time going back to school. My gap year before getting my master's degree accidentally turned into three. Having this job so quickly after getting out of school is my dream come true. I guess I'm still eager to prove that I deserve this job. I'm still not sure how to fit a personal life alongside my career."

Angie pushed, "There's no time like the present to try and make that balance happen."

"You're right. Thanks for showing me the ropes."

Angie groaned as she chewed off another monstrous bite of pastry, "You're more than just your professional work."

"Be nice, I'm still learning how to juggle."

Angie quipped, "If you're holding one thing then you're not juggling."

Madison sent a small nod in Angie's direction. Angie tossed her head back and laughed. Her long black locks bounced against her shoulders as her healthy tan skin shone in the afternoon sun. The sunny but cool day hinted at what was to come as winter slowly tightened its grip around Lakewood.

"Thanks, Angie."

"Don't mention it, M. Look, you're still here! Our boss loves you and you're doing a great job. Keep your chin up. Have you thought about what you want to do since you've been here?"

Angie leisurely swirled the last bite of pastry against the bottom of her plate as she waited for a reply. She was like an overactive vacuum whenever anything sugary was involved. Angie effortlessly kept a curvaceous hourglass figure with perfectly placed curves. She looked great in anything.

The question caught Madison mid-sip. Her coffee cup halted in the air as her lips blew over the piping chocolatey sludge. It was a little too late in the afternoon for another coffee. She didn't mind having another cup whenever she wanted to stay up past her typical bedtime. But on an uneventful work night? Not so much.

Madison's brows pulled together as she mulled over Angie's question. Eventually, she answered, "Honestly, I haven't had time to map out a real direction for anything besides my career. My dream is to be a quality reporter with a dedicated news segment. Eventually, I want to become an anchor, but it all feels so abstract. I promised myself that I would hone my talent, but it just feels so out of reach."

"Maybe write it down? To be fair, success is subjective, Hon. You're so much closer than 10 or even five years ago. It's all about perspective. Besides, you're more than just a career. You're everything that makes you shine."

"So you want me to write my career goals in a journal? I don't have a journal."

"No, M. Write down all of the things that you've wanted to accomplish since moving to Lakewood. Think of it like an adult version of a Christmas list. Accomplishing everything on your list before Saint Nick arrives at the end of the month is probably ambitious, but you get the idea. It's supposed to be a positive challenge."

"That's a good idea. Maybe I can make a dent in this adult-Christmas list later tonight."

Angie stirred her nearly empty coffee. She kept her eyes glued to the liquid as she asked, "Want to give me the headline?"

"What if I write down fostering more relationships?"

"That's a start. We have a massive Christmas Festival coming up and I can introduce you to a few young people in town. Technically, it's a fundraiser for the local school, but Lakewood likes to find any excuse to celebrate."

Madison waved her hand through the air, "I was thinking more along the lines of getting a pet."

Angie blinked.

Sensing her friend's confusion, she added, "I've always wanted a pet."

Madison knew it wasn't the same as getting to know the people in town. Still, maybe adopting a pet would help her to feel more settled. As her mom always said, the first step to growing roots was deciding to plant a tree.

To her credit, Angie seemed mostly unfazed. She cleared her throat and added, "That could work. It's always nice to check things off a list. I guess the top of the list will include your next food-related news segment?"

"You guessed it. We're heading over to cover a piece about Bobby's Pizzeria."

"That's right! Bobby's Pizzeria has been around for decades. I can't believe it's in danger of closing right before the busy season. It doesn't make sense. Bobby's wife is the best accountant in town. If anyone can run a business, it's her."

"I'll get the full scoop later this week. I'm bummed that I never got to try a slice. Weren't they famous for their deep dish pepperoni pies?"

"Iconic. Always had a line at least six people deep," Angie waved a hand and mimicked a line of people stretching for miles on end. The sleeves of her light pink pantsuit bunched as she made a few jerky movements.

Madison huffed and tapped her fingers along the corner of the table. The bell above the small bakery's door happily chimed as patrons came and went. She wondered if the place ever experienced a lull in foot traffic. Probably not. It was located directly in the middle of town.

A handful of construction fences erected across the street hinted at the upcoming skate park. Pretty soon, the place would be packed with people eager for a snack between skating sessions. It wasn't lost on Madison how everyone in Lakewood loved to skateboard or ice skate. She felt like every adult in the area knew how to ice skate. The skate park in the center of town spoke to the younger generation with half-pipes and ramps designed for a more land-loving approach. Still, the nearest ice skating pond was only a five-minute walk away from the center of town. Madison thought it was like having the best of both worlds.

Angie flicked a few strands of dark wavy hair away from her face as she looked out the window. Christmas was one of the busiest times of the year. Her brows pulled together as she returned her attention back to the conversation.

Angie was a handful of years older than Madison. The small age gap made Madison feel like she was somehow seeing into the future. A path just out of sight. She wondered if Angie's extra years spent within the industry helped her to find her center.

Madison appreciated having a friend who was so grounded and hardworking. If only she could find a way to make friends with people outside of her job. Maybe that could go on her adult Christmas list.

She noticed Angie's tensed jaw and frowned. It wasn't normal for Angie to look so upset. Between the two, Madison held the record by complaining about anything and everything under the sun.

"What's wrong, Angie? We've spent most of our lunch break talking about me. How is your son, Max?"

Angie waved her pastry-covered hand in the air, "Max is such a sweet kid, but public speaking really isn't in his comfort zone. His dinosaur diorama presentation didn't go as well as we had hoped. His teacher said he grew flustered and sat back down in the middle of his presentation."

"Oh, no! I'm sorry, Angie! I know you and Max spent hours working on his speech. It sounded perfect when Max presented it to me in your kitchen."

"That's because he likes you, Madison. He isn't as confident around kids his own age and it doesn't help that he tends to stutter."

Madison's face pinched with empathy. She hoped Max would be able to pass with flying colors on the next assignment. Better yet, maybe the teacher would let Max redo his dinosaur presentation. He knew the material like the back of his hand. Max just needed someone willing to help him shine.

"I'm sorry, Angie. Maybe there is a way to help him overcome his fear of public speaking?"

Madison reached out and squeezed her friend's hand. She knew Angie was overwhelmed. Her husband had been stuck out of the country on a business trip for longer than expected. Something about bad weather and frozen plane engines. Madison had a sneaking suspicion that the current long-distance strained their relationship. Max was just the kind of kid perceptive enough to notice such changes within his household.

Angie groaned, "I've been looking for a way to help Max. I search the internet every night before going to bed like some compulsive routine. Every night, I get home from work and search for ways to build his confidence and help with school. I'd give anything to help my little boy."

Madison squeezed Angie's hand. Angie had taken Madison under her wing and taught her everything she needed to know about their quaint local news station. As the newest and youngest reporter in the office, she appreciated a friendly smile and a helpful nudge while getting up to speed.

Madison wanted to be there for her new friend. She didn't have the heart to tell Angie that she had also searched the internet high and low for public speaking tips. The irony of the situation hadn't escaped her. They both held careers centered around public speaking, but couldn't figure out how to impart their knowledge to a child.

"Angie!" The barista hollered over the crowd as he held one large hot coffee with extra foam above the sea of bobbing heads.

"We can look online together. Here, let me grab your coffee."

Madison pointed at Angie's cup and headed over to the counter. She placed her hand on the counter filled to the brim with to-go orders. The number of orders felt immense. Were there really this many people living in Lakewood?

The barista smiled, "Back again?"

"Absolutely. This one is for Angie."

"Here you are."

"Thank you." Madison smiled at the barista. She turned around just as a massive wall slammed into her relatively short frame.

Hot coffee slopped against the front of Madison's shirt. Luckily, it was only a few drops. Madison looked down and sighed with relief. A few splotches dotted the right sleeve of her shirt. The small mess wasn't anything that a thorough scrub couldn't fix. Relieved, Madison looked up and winced.

The wall turned out to be a handsome man in his early thirties. He stared at Madison with shockingly blue eyes filled with dismay.

The front of his shirt looked as if he had finished a mud race. The once pristine blue button-up now donned a spreading brown smear near the center. The crotch of his pants had managed to take the brunt of the foam.

Madison puckered her lower lip as her brown doe eyes looked up into shocked ocean orbs. Mortification threatened to swallow Madison alive. Red crept up the base of her neck as she practically sprinted over to one of the tables and yanked several napkins out of a holder.

"Napkins! I am so sorry. Use these to soak up some of the cream or maybe the coffee? How about both?"

Madison handed the poor man a wad of paper napkins. She wanted to help but refrained. She figured pawing at a complete stranger in the middle of a public coffee shop wasn't exactly the way to make a positive first impression.

"Thank you. Don't worry, I bobbed when you weaved."

"You're a professional fighter?" Madison tilted her head to the side and tried to picture the handsome stranger fighting. Something about his calm and collected nature hinted at the possibility. She studied his features and noted his regal Roman nose. His assertive jaw and broad shoulders hinted at a different occupation.

"No, I own a restaurant down the road. My dad was a boxer before he owned the restaurant."

"Oh, that's amazing. Here, take my business card. Let me pay for the dry cleaning bill. It's the least that I can do."

Madison reached into her pocket and pulled out her new business card. Her fingers caressed the top of the stranger's palm as he deftly accepted the card.

"You work for Channel 40 News?"

"Yes, I recently moved here from New York. I'm covering local stories all around town so it won't be any trouble for me to pay for the ruined clothes."

"You don't need to pay for my dry cleaning. Accidents happen."

"Oh, I really do. It's my first Christmas in town and I can't be known as the accident-prone new girl. This is my first outing in days and I've already dropped a scalding drink onto a stranger."

"Your secret is safe with me, Madison."

The stranger read over her business card for a second time while the corners of his lips quirked up into a teasing smile.

"It was nice to meet you." Madison's sentence hung in the air once she realized she didn't know the stranger's name. Who was the mystery man she'd scalded with caffeinated water?

"Vincent. I know a place you can hide until this public debacle dies down. Half of the town likes to stop by Sweetie's Bakery for breakfast. Luckily, it happened during the morning rush so everyone's too busy to care.

Stop by DeLuca's Restaurant after work and you can try a more pasta-oriented menu."

"That's a dangerous offer. I love pasta."

Madison imagined a menu full of the best homemade Italian food that the town had to offer. Secretly, she craved the comfort offered by a large home-cooked meal. Unfortunately, her work schedule was often so hectic that she barely had the time or the energy to microwave leftovers.

"A challenge that I'm happy to accept. See you around, Madison."

Vincent revealed a heart-stopping smile as he waved goodbye and headed out the door.

Madison settled back into her wooden seat as a faint blush crept up along her pale cheeks. She felt like her head was in the clouds as she sat back down.

Angie arched her brow, "What happened to the coffee?"

Chapter 2

"This is Madison Crawford and I am reporting to you live from the newly renovated skate park located in the heart of downtown Lakewood. As you can see, the skate park has turned out to be a huge success thanks to three different half-pipes and a wide paved space that's perfect for skateboarders eager to hone their skills. Local businesses claim that the new addition to the neighborhood has already boosted foot traffic and increased sales. I'm Madison Crawford and this is Channel 40 News."

As the camera lights turned off, Madison lowered the microphone away from her face. Her heart pounded with excitement. A small smile illuminated her features as she basked in the glow of an uplifting story. The story was a bit of a softball, but Madison was happy to take it one step at a time. It was a step above getting stuck with office paperwork.

Madison knew she'd need to offer her boss an exciting story if she wanted to stand out from the crowd. Stories about skate parks and bakeries were nice, but she knew she needed to do something more.

"Cut! That was perfect, Madison. Want to grab a snack before starting the next story? I'm hungry."

Lenny called from behind the massive camera as he searched the surrounding restaurants like a starved man in the middle of a buffet. His portly belly protruded against his snug jeans. A light layer of sweat covered his face as he waited for Madison to reply.

"Thanks, Lenny. I'm not very hungry so go ahead without me. I'm going to finish up a few emails and take a short walk."

"Sounds like a plan." Lenny shrugged his burly shoulders and then packed up the remaining equipment. Madison helped put a few lighter items into the news truck before Lenny made a beeline for downtown's restaurant row.

Madison stretched her legs and took advantage of the nice weather as she finished up a few emails in the warmer-than-usual sunshine. She kept the news van in sight as she settled onto a bench only a few paces away.

In truth, the emails weren't that important. Madison just wanted to have a minute alone. She didn't want to admit it, but she felt awkward filming around town. In a place where everyone knew everyone for generations, the title of newcomer left her with few places to hide.

Madison decided she needed to get over the discomfort. She'd babied her newcomer status for too long and was starting to look unapproachable. Not a good look for someone whose entire job depends on interacting with the public. It was ironic that making new friends felt like such a struggle. In an odd way, Madison felt like the new kid in school.

She looked away from her phone screen and scanned the downtown area. Madison still had a little over an hour before the next broadcast. That was just enough time to explore.

She sent Lenny a quick text explaining she was going to stretch her legs. Within seconds, he replied with a quick thumbs-up emoji and a pizza emoji. Madison fought the urge to roll her eyes. She knew Lenny was sweet, but sometimes she felt like she was guessing when it came to texting him. Thanks to his young daughter, his messages often included more pictures than words. Luckily, this one seemed easy enough to decipher: sounds good; I'm having pizza.

Massive fake snowflakes and elaborate green wreaths covered the front of the nearest store. She looked down the row and found one festive shop after the next. Lakewood sure loved to get into the holiday spirit. The unusually warm weather felt at odds with the season. Sure, New York was a smidge higher up on the map, but Colorado surely had a few cold moments, right?

She kept her attention glued to the storefronts as her feet took the sidewalk in stride. Madison stopped outside of a sleepy restaurant with only a handful of elderly patrons. She cupped her hands over her face and tried to catch a glimpse inside. The tables and chairs were clean and the dishes looked immaculate, but for some reason, the image reminded Madison of a doll house. The lack of people made it feel more like a fantasy than an actual place to hunker down for a nice hearty meal.

The spotless window lacked the holiday spirit practically bursting out from the other establishments. It was like Scrooge himself had decided to make a restaurant.

Madison's phone buzzed. She didn't recognize the number and contemplated ignoring the call. On a whim, she answered. Of course, curiosity had a way of killing the cat.

She swiped her finger against the screen and answered, "Hello?"

Chapter 3

"Are you hungry?"

The voice held a husky quality that sounded oddly familiar. Madison squinted as she tried to place where she had heard it before.

Confused, Madison pressed the phone closer to her ear as she turned around and searched the crowd walking along Main Street for a familiar face. A few kids with flame-colored helmets and shiny new skateboards rolled in the general direction of the new skate park. The throaty chuckle on the opposite end of the phone betrayed the mystery caller's identity. A playful grin crossed Madison's face as she tried to locate the person laughing on the other line.

Motion inside the joyless restaurant grabbed Madison's attention. Her eyes locked with Vincent's as he held up his phone. He waved and motioned for her to come inside.

Madison's eyes momentarily drank in his attire. She appreciated how his pink apron and rolled-up shirt sleeves accentuated his toned muscles. She drew in a deep gulp of air and struggled to remain composed.

Easier said than done.

She pushed open the glass door while still holding her phone next to her ear. Maybe she'd be able to write a story about the restaurant.

"Did I find DeLuca's?"

Madison tilted her head as her voice echoed through the phone line. She ended the call and stepped inside.

"On your first try," Vincent's face broke into a pleased smirk as Madison removed her light coat and looked around the room. The warmth thawed her slightly chilled fingers. Although the temperature was mild for the start of December, it was still cold enough to require a jacket.

The bright red brick walls were covered with proudly displayed black and white pictures of customers from a not-so-distant past. The photos hung above a few checkered booths with a small mirror breaking up the sea of monochrome smiles. The back of the dining area revealed a modernized open-concept kitchen. Madison could tell that a ton of time and money had been spent remodeling the interior.

DeLuca's was a diamond in the rough. The sophisticated touches inside of the restaurant felt like well-hidden treasures. However, one pressing detail stood out like a sore thumb as Madison looked around the room. Her eyes narrowed as she noticed the complete absence of Christmas decorations. For a town so committed to festivities, it appeared that Madison had found the unlikely resident Scrooge. The edges of Madison's lips threatened to quirk into a smile.

Unwilling to start on a negative note, she instead chose to break the ice with a genuine compliment. "This place looks amazing! Did you just redo the kitchen?"

Vincent chuckled, but his handsome features didn't exactly light up with joy. He answered, "I guess you could say that. The place was gutted and remodeled about two months ago, but it doesn't seem like anyone's even noticed. That's why everything looks so new. It's barely been used."

"That's a shame." Madison frowned as she walked around the room and inspected the shining plates and pristine tables. Vincent casually leaned against the counter, clad in a neon pink apron. The pop of color looked equal parts fitting and ridiculous.

She walked to the back of the restaurant and peeked into the cutting-edge kitchen. Madison noticed a few freshly chopped vegetables on the counter and asked, "Were you preparing for the dinner crowd?"

Vincent laughed, "I was hoping for one or two guests. I wouldn't exactly call that a dinner rush. Here, try some."

He waved Madison over and lifted the divider so that she could enter the kitchen first. Madison ducked under his arm and entered the polished space.

"Thanks."

The kitchen smelt delicious. A handful of pots simmered over low fires. Curiosity got the better of her as she walked over and inspected the stovetop.

Madison's hand hovered above one of the lids, "May I?"

Vincent nodded, "Inspect away."

"Consider it an impromptu visit from the health department."

"By all means, check every corner." Vincent nodded his head and smirked. His confident demeanor set Madison at ease as she carefully lifted one of the lids.

"Oh, wow! Beef stew! My mom used to make me this when I was a kid. It was my favorite thing to eat after a long day on the ice."

"On the ice?"

"Yes, I used to ice skate in New York. Hopefully, I'll be able to keep up that hobby. I noticed the new skate park but haven't found the time to go to the pond."

Vincent laughed, "The skate park is a great addition to the town. It will keep the kiddos busy in the summer while they wait for the ice to return."

"Is everyone in town dedicated to sports?"

Vincent shrugged, "I never thought of it that way. We have a lot of traditions centered around playing and eating. Maybe Lakewood can be considered the best of both worlds."

"If that's true, I should start working on my ice skating. I'm excited to see my first holiday snowstorm."

"I wouldn't hold my breath for that."

"Why not?"

"People say the town of Lakewood is cursed. We haven't had a snowy Christmas in over 100 years. The last time it snowed my great-great-grandfather had just opened this place."

"That sounds like a long curse."

"Legend has it that the mayor of this town broke a beautiful witch's heart right before Christmas. The man the witch fell in love with was too proud to apologize for his wrongs. His pride thawed the witch's love for him. In return for the heartbreak, the beautiful witch vowed it would never snow on Christmas. A curse that's lasted over 100 years."

"That's some curse," Madison paused as she took in Vincent's small grin. Wait a minute.

She pressed, "Vincent, you wouldn't happen to be related to this heartbreaking mayor?"

"You don't miss a thing. Yes, the mayor in the story is a distant relative of mine. He was a stubborn man, more interested in his restaurant and mayoral duties than following his heart. The DeLuca men are known for being stubborn. I think it's more of a pride issue."

"Is that why you haven't decorated the restaurant for Christmas? Are you on strike?"

Vincent huffed as he dipped a small spoon into one of the pots and gently blew on the spoonful of beef stew. He extended the spoon and arched a brow in Madison's direction.

"Would you like to taste the final product, Inspector?"

Madison closed her mouth around the spoon and groaned. It tasted just like her mother's recipe. A pang of nostalgia danced inside of her chest.

"It's delicious."

Satisfied, Vincent poured a generous serving into a bowl. Eventually, he admitted, "I'm not superstitious. Legends are the stories we like to tell each other when huddled around the fireplace to pass the time. I didn't decorate DeLuca's this year because there isn't much to celebrate."

"What do you mean?"

Vincent paused as he weighed his options. After a beat, he admitted, "People aren't coming to the restaurant like they used to. If things keep heading in the same direction, then it looks like we'll need to close right after the holidays. Right now, I don't even have enough money to afford a full-time staff."

"That doesn't make any sense. Your food is delicious." Madison wiped the corners of her lips as she enjoyed another spoonful of the freshly made stew. How could a place this delicious be so easily forgotten?

"Thanks, I just wish that the town felt the same way. Restaurants keep closing down and I'm afraid DeLuca's might be next." Vincent served himself a larger portion and leaned back against the wall. His usually electric blue eyes seemed clouded with sadness as he stared off into the distance. His soulful orbs stood out against his dark neatly trimmed hair. He looked more suited to taking over a boardroom than commanding an empty kitchen.

"Maybe we need to remind the town about your delicious food. People don't always know what they like until it's right in front of them."

"You make a good point."

"Of course, I do."

Madison glanced at her phone and realized that she needed to hurry back to Lenny. She didn't want to run late.

Madison sighed, "I'm still on the clock. Can we talk more another time? I'm free tomorrow."

"Sure," Vincent pulled out his phone and furiously typed out a message.

Madison's phone chimed.

Vincent noticed the questioning look drawn across Madison's face. He answered, "Now you have my number."

"And now you have at least one loyal customer." Madison reached into her purse and pulled out her wallet.

"It's on the house," Vincent moved back and refused to take her money.

Madison playfully narrowed her eyes, "Consider the money payment for your ruined shirt. If you don't take the money then you're rewarding me for ruining your clothing."

Vincent shrugged, "It was old. Besides, I'm wearing an apron because I had a feeling you were coming."

He sent her a playful wink.

"Very funny."

Madison sucked in her lower lip and hid her smile. After so many years in a bustling metropolitan city, she knew how to spot quality clothing. Vincent's shirt and pants had been expensive, to say the least. He easily shrugged off her offer to pay him back with an innocent white lie. A white lie she recognized but didn't want to ruin. She'd find a way to pay him back.

"Thank you for the stew. See you tomorrow." Madison waved at Vincent and headed to the front door. With her back turned to the kitchen, Madison shuffled out her wallet. She paused and placed several dollar bills on the table closest to the door.

A displeased yell rang from the back of the kitchen. That was her cue.
Before Vincent could catch her, Madison sped out of the restaurant and shouted, "I still owe you!"

The door closed as Vincent yelled an unintelligible sentence. Something told Madison that Vincent was saying something along the lines of *you're not getting away with this.*

Madison returned to the news truck with a bounce in her step. She wondered why Vincent's restaurant had such a people problem as she prepared to finish her shift.

Chapter 4

Madison couldn't get her impromptu lunch with Vincent out of her head. Her cheeks flushed as her mind replayed how effortlessly Vincent moved around his kitchen. It was as if he knew every inch of the newly remodeled kitchen. Most likely because he did.

"Where's your head?"

Lenny's thick New Jersey accent drawled as he hefted the camera equipment higher onto his shoulder. He easily kept pace with Madison even with several pounds of gear attempting to weigh him down. Lenny was as strong as an ox with a healthy appetite to boot.

"Nowhere, I'm just thinking about all of the restaurants that I haven't tried."

Lenny joked, "You better hurry up or you'll miss out."

Madison frowned, "What does that mean?"

"Haven't you noticed? Almost every week a restaurant is either permanently closing or getting into trouble with the health department."

Madison held open the door as Lenny bustled inside the location of their upcoming story. He lowered his voice and whispered, "It's the end of Lakewood's dining scene. That's all I'm gonna say about it."

Madison frowned as she mulled over Lenny's timely words. They were just about to do a piece on Bobby's Pizzeria. The business was a well-loved staple within the community. According to Lenny and Angie, the pizzeria had the best slice of pie in town.

The restaurant was only a few paces away from the new skate park which acted as a sprawling divider between the two sides of the street.

A short man with balding hair bustled around the clean plastic tables and chairs. He hurried over with his hand outstretched. A few beads of sweat dampened his collared shirt.

He hollered, "Welcome to Bobby's Pizzeria! I'm Bobby."

Madison reached out and shook the owner's hand. His brows pulled together as he attempted to look relaxed. Lenny's earlier words danced in the back of her mind. How badly was Bobby's Pizzeria struggling? Madison wondered if there was a reason why all of the eateries in town were suddenly experiencing trouble. Maybe there was a real mystery lurking right under her nose.

"Please come in. It's good to see you, Lenny. My wife is usually around, but she's visiting our eldest son today."

Lenny shrugged as he set up the camera. He grunted, "I told you I was coming back, Bobby. Tell the missus I said hi."

"Right, but I didn't know you meant so soon!"

Madison checked over the microphone as recognition dawned across her features. Lenny came to Bobby's Pizzeria on his lunch break.

Indecision danced in Madison's chest. Why wasn't she more outgoing? Wouldn't it help her career to make more of an effort? She made a mental note to make her adult Christmas List as soon as her shift ended. Becoming more settled in Lakewood was inching straight to the top of her wish list. More like her holiday to-do list.

"Where would you like to start?"

Bobby spread his arms out as he gestured to the wide-spanning pizzeria. The cramped kitchen in the back was safely tucked behind a counter littered with toppled to-go boxes. Madison spun in a slow, deliberate circle and contemplated the perfect background. A small window near the front of the shop caught her eye. It looked like a tiny to-go area with the perfect sliding glass window. The window tilted to the right. Madison wondered if the wonky design had anything to do with the odd angle of the slanted building. She knew that most of the older buildings were at least 100 years old. It wasn't surprising to learn that the more established locations came with a few quirks.

"Is that a to-go window?"

An irritated look crossed Bobby's face as he jabbed his thick finger in the direction of the window and grumbled, "The scene of the crime!"

Madison watched Bobby's face and tried to understand if the man reaching right below her shoulder was serious. Was this restaurant owner a prankster? Madison looked at Lenny, and the two exchanged glances. Lenny shrugged and returned to fiddling with the camera equipment before anyone could catch their exchange. Madison took the noncommittal gesture to mean that Bobby was serious (in his own way).

"Would you like to tell us more?"

Bobby huffed, "Sure."

He headed straight for the to-go window like a torpedo locked onto an unsuspecting target. Bam! Bobby slapped his hand against the bottom of the window and announced, "Madison, you'll get the story before the news. I just had this baby installed. Sure, it's not exactly a looker, but it gets the job done. The window opens and closes to keep out the weather and the speaker helps communicate order numbers to hungry to-go customers. I thought a pizza slice to-go window would really bump up sales with the new skate park just a few steps away. Talk about changing with the times. I remember when skateboarding was just starting to get popular."

Madison could feel Bobby digressing. She nudged, "What about the window?"

"The window is the entire reason I'm in this mess! Someone called the local health department and said the window was one inch shorter than regulation standards. It's also crooked and violates some other city code. Do you want to know the real kicker? The town approved the plans. We worked for months getting the permits and making sure everything was right. Last month, I got a visit from an inspector with bad news. Now, Bobby's Pizzeria must fix the issues and also pay multiple fines."

Madison empathized with Bobby. He put in a lot of effort to have it go down the drain. She thought the timing of the inspector was odd. Why would a city health inspector return to a place out of the blue?

She absently tapped her fingers along the edges of her microphone. It was turned off. Since Lenny was still setting up the shot, Madison knew she had enough time to ask a few more questions before the broadcast started.

"Isn't it normal for health inspectors to visit without any warning?"

Bobby slapped the side of the window like an overwhelmed car salesman. He huffed, "Sure, but not like this. Do you want to know the real kicker? I'll tell you. Someone called and made an anonymous complaint with the local departments. It doesn't make any sense! I thought the plans were perfect but suddenly everything was wrong. This is going to really set the business back. I'll be lucky if we can even stay open with all of the unexpected expenses."

Madison coughed as she contemplated what Bobby was saying. His pinched brows and reddened cheeks highlighted his frustration. He looked halfway between starting a screaming match and bursting into tears.

"We'll share your story with the town, Bobby. I'm so sorry this happened. Would it be okay if we got the to-go window in the shot?"

Bobby nodded his head so quickly that he momentarily looked like a bobblehead. He shuffled back to Madison and looked between her and Lenny.

"Just tell me where I need to stand, Kiddo."

Chapter 5

"You'll never guess what I just learned."

Angie murmured on the opposite end of the phone. The distant laughter of children told Madison that her friend was busy picking up Max from school.

"Let me guess, you have no idea how to complete your reasonable adult Christmas list before Christmas?" Angie's voice rang on a pitch-perfect high note as she waited for Madison to respond.

"Funny. I have a few ideas for my Christmas list. So far it feels way less exciting than Max's list, but that's not the point. The point is I just interviewed Bobby from Bobby's Pizzeria. He said a few things that made me think that Lakewood might have a mystery cooking."

"Way to bury the lead!"

"I didn't! You derailed the conversation," Madison huffed as she drove home for the day. Her earlier talk with Bobby kept replaying in the back of her mind like a broken record. She figured it was only fair to fill Angie in on the news. While the news story didn't hint at the possible mystery, it did cover Bobby's recent code violation woes. The story instantly grabbed Madison's interest. She sensed a few dots starting to connect between Bobby's Pizzeria and DeLuca's Restaurant. Two restaurants with over thirty years of experience are suddenly in danger of being closed within the same year? Madison knew enough to recognize when something smelled fishy.

Chatter filled the opposite end of the phone call as Angie greeted a few parents from Max's grade. Madison was sure the conversation would need to be fast. How long did it take a kid to get out of school? Angie tried to keep business separate from her home life. Madison guessed she had a few more minutes to catch her friend up to speed before Max came racing out of school.

"Okay, listen. Bobby said that someone anonymously reported his restaurant to the health department."

"That doesn't make any sense! His place is so clean you can practically eat off the floor. I wouldn't recommend it, but you get the point."

"Right. I thought the same thing. Apparently, someone reported the size and slant of his new to-go window. It's not up to code. Bobby insists the department approved the window. Now he's stuck trying to come back from the hefty fines. He might even need to redo the entire window. Bobby was hoping to use the sales made off the new skate park's foot traffic to recoup the loss. Even if he catches up with the fines and expenses, he'll still be behind."

"You think it's a big if. The expenses must be bad. Bobby never complains."

Madison sighed as she pulled up to her cozy cabin. It was a few miles away from the heart of town. When she'd accepted the job, she thought it would be a great idea to save a few dollars and live in the heart of the forest. The rent was reasonable, plus Madison enjoyed the generously sized back porch. It also helped that the woodsy furniture was included.

Madison hopped out of the car and replied, "Yep. I think the news story might get a bit of foot traffic to his shop but it's still not enough. He seemed to be in a tight spot."

Angie sighed, "I hope he's able to hold on a little longer. Bobby's Pizzeria has a great location, especially now that the local skate park opened up. Tons of locals are buzzing about and looking for their next quick bite to eat."

"Exactly!"

Max's voice rang through the phone as he greeted his mom. A small smile tugged at the corners of Madison's lips as she opened her finicky front door. She worried that the tight lock was bound to get stuck one of these days.

"Hi Max!"

"Madison says hi," Angie conveyed to Max.

The call was slowly coming to an end, but Madison couldn't find it in herself to hang up. She wanted to feel connected to other people for just a few more minutes. The gentle sounds of the forest creatures were nice, but sometimes Madison craved a little something more.

"Can I call you later? Max just reached the pickup line."

Time's up.

A ghost of a smile thinned her lips as she replied, "Sure. Talk soon."

Madison sighed and looked around the first floor of her compact home. She couldn't believe she'd lived in the same space for almost a full six months. The furnished rental had everything that she could ask for from a proper coffee maker to a generous collection of mystery novels neatly stacked near the working fireplace.

Maybe she needed to take a look at her list. A quick glance at her phone said that it was the middle of the afternoon. Surely, most of the stores in town were still open. Right?

The wooden floors creaked as Madison ascended the stairs to her room. She settled at her desk and read the first few items on her list. Her to-do list before Christmas felt vastly less exciting compared to Max's. Madison knew her list was nothing compared to a traditional Christmas wish list, but she figured it still counted.

Madison whispered her list out loud. "Take more photos, adopt a pet, put down roots, get a promotion."

She wrinkled her nose. How was she supposed to accomplish everything on her list before the end of the holiday season? Feeling hopeful, Madison wrote down one item she hoped would be easier to make come true.

"Eat a homemade apple pie."

Madison grinned as she imagined Angie scouring the stores the week before Christmas. Given Angie's love of organization, it wouldn't be a shock if she had already shopped several months in advance for the holiday season. Angie probably had everything purchased and wrapped since the first day of August.

"Put down roots."

Madison huffed. She tossed the sheet of paper back onto her desk. Putting down roots? Why didn't she just ask for the world? The two felt about the same. Madison rubbed her head and wondered if she needed to break down the goal into smaller pieces. Maybe she needed to get a pet. She had a regular schedule and had the funds to support a pet. Madison hummed as she thought of reasonable ideal pets for a first-time pet owner. She opened her phone and searched for the nearest adoption center.

She looked out the window and noticed the sun was still high in the sky. Madison decided to seize the moment. She sprinted down the stairs and lazily locked the pesky front door. Nothing bad ever happened in a small town, right?

Chapter 6

Most of the cages at the animal shelter were empty. Madison wasn't sure what she had expected, but the unoccupied cages and sterile white walls weren't it. To her surprise, the front cages were full of puppies. What were the odds that everyone in Lakewood would want to drive all the way to Waverly to adopt a pet? Madison considered adopting a puppy but thought otherwise. She wanted to help a creature less likely to get a second chance.

The woman at the front desk walked over. Her scuffed white sneakers echoed along the tiled hallway. She clicked a pen in her right hand as she greeted, "We like to call it a lull before the holiday season. It has its pros and cons. Hopefully, most of the pets will get adopted and stay adopted well after the holiday buzz."

Madison looked down the rows as her shoulders slumped with disappointment. It was a small hiccup, but for some reason, Madison also felt like it was a sign. She didn't want a puppy because puppies were the easiest to adopt. Maybe she could adopt an older dog or a pet that was not always first on everyone's list.

The woman's statement piqued Madison's curiosity. She turned her attention away from the cages and asked, "What do you mean after the holiday buzz?"

The woman pointed a few cages down. "We usually have people that adopt a pet without thinking about it as a long-term commitment. Pets aren't toys. The puppy phase doesn't last."

"How often are the younger cats and dogs adopted?"

"Almost every day."

"We're having a clear the shelter event in the next few weeks. This year, we hope to have all of our animals adopted by loving families before the end of Christmas Day."

"That's a big goal."

The other woman sighed as she tapped the side of her scuffed white shoe against the floor. She looked over at Madison and noted, "Yeah. We're always looking for better ways to spread the word."

Madison nodded as she looked around the shelter. She knew adopting a pet would be a challenge. That was a given. Madison wanted to tell the adoption center worker she worked for the local news but stopped short. She worried about making false promises. Madison figured it was better to pitch the idea before saying anything to the animal shelter. With a little bit of broadcasting magic, every single animal would have a warm place to call home, just in time for the holiday season.

A distant memory danced in the back of her mind. Pets were an extension of the family. At least that's what Madison's father, living far away in a sprawling New York estate, liked to say about his Golden Retrievers.

Madison thanked the woman at the shelter and slowly turned around. Her steps sounded muted as she tentatively shuffled across the tiled floor. The woman from the front desk had already sped away to help another eager potential adopter. Maybe Madison should have called ahead instead of driving over to the shelter in such a rush. The situation was bittersweet. Still, Madison wanted to find her own companion. So far, the odds weren't in her favor.

A sharp vibration tugged Madison away from her negative train of thought. She pulled out a hair tie and a book while on her way to rescue her phone from the bottomless pit of her purse. Notepads and pens floated away from her grasp as she trawled near several handfuls of discarded pennies for her phone. She wondered why her boss was calling her on her time off. Then again, Jannie always called her to pick up missing shifts. As a recent newcomer, Madison was like a moving target when it came to picking up the slack. Still, she liked her job and didn't mind the extra money. Madison made a mental note to pitch Jannie a holiday special dedicated to the animal shelter.

"Odd," Madison arched a brow as Angie's name flitted across her screen.

"Hello?"

Distant static crackled from the opposite end of the phone. Angie's voice mumbled a garbled sentence. The hairs on the back of Madison's neck stood on end as she listened to the frustration in her friend's voice.

"Angie?"

Another crackle crossed the line before Angie replied, "Hi, M. Max brought home the class pet for the weekend. Would you believe the class pet had babies? I agreed to help with the pet calendar before the babies came into the picture. Could you please come over? I know it's a lot to ask, but I don't know what to do. Max opened the cage so now tiny little creatures are running all over the house!"

Angie's usually collected and posh tone ended on a high note. It sounded closer to a squawk as Max giggled in the background. At least one member of the Landerson household was having a blast.

"Sure, I'll be right over." Madison hopped into the front seat of her blue car. The shiny new vehicle glimmered in the dying light. If Madison had looked in her rearview mirror, she would have seen a slim figure retreating into the bushes only a few paces away from her parked car.

Chapter 7

Winding multi-colored plastic tubes caught Madison's eye. She inched closer as a few little black and brown poofs came into view. Little noses twitched as Madison's light perfume announced her arrival.

"What do we have here?"

Angie huffed, "Apparently my weekend plans. Max says this is going to be the best weekend ever. I thought this class pet business would be a breeze. Now, I'm starting to regret not getting him a puppy."

"Hi, Aunt Madison!"

Max wiggled out from behind the sofa. His hair stuck out in every direction imaginable, but his clothes still looked remarkably clean. Madison was willing to bet he changed his outfit after the hamster fiasco that Angie had explained over the phone. Madison was glad she didn't have to wash that out.

"Hi, Max! How do you like the pet-sitting business?"

"It's great. Look at the little guys. They're so cute." Max pointed at the ambling fluff balls as they roamed around their multi-level enclosure.

Angie gave Madison a glance over the top of Max's head that said something along the lines of: he gets to have a great time while I go out of my mind trying to keep all of these little pom poms alive.

Tiny fingers wrapped around Madison's wrist as Max brought her over to the metallic cage. It looked like a deluxe jungle gym with all of the whirling tunnels and brightly colored multi-level ladders.

The contraption vaguely reminded Madison of her childhood. She remembered begging her parents to visit the jungle gyms at her favorite fast-food restaurant. The ladders and plastic-colored tunnels were so much fun. During the lunch rush, the warm sun reflected off the plastic walls and turned the world into a kaleidoscope of brightly colored possibilities.

Max placed a small finger into the cage and added in a voice just above a whisper, "Aren't they the cutest?"

"Here, this is their bag of treats," Max hesitantly pulled out a bag of tiny pellets. He gave Madison a generous handful and nodded at the hamsters. He bounced on the heels of his feet as he waited to see Madison's reaction.

Madison pushed a piece of hair behind her ear as she leaned over the cage. She looked inside the enclosure and noticed a tiny black furry body nestled behind the other fur balls.

"I like the one in the back. Can I see the little opal hamster?"

Max blinked. He looked at his mom for approval before carefully opening the top of the enclosure. His practiced movements spoke volumes about the previous hamster escape. Max took his time as he reached inside the cage. After a few minutes, a black ball of fur appeared from the fluffy chaos.

Madison carefully held out her hands as the tiny creature nuzzled into her palms. She listened to the pint-sized snuffles and grinned.

"What's this hamster's name?"

"We haven't gotten around to naming them. He's the runt of the litter and we weren't sure he would make it without enough attention.

The teacher says that the babies are up for adoption.”

The statement pulled on Madison’s heartstrings as she raised her hands closer to her face. This little animal was nothing like the one she had anticipated adopting at the shelter. His little fluffy body easily fit inside the palm of her hand. As she held the little hamster, she could see two curious bright eyes staring back at her.

“You just need a chance. It’s okay, Rocko. You’ll like my house.”

Angie laughed, “Really? I thought you wanted to get a dog?”

Madison grumbled, “Sometimes the world tells you what you need.”

“Is the world telling you to get a hamster?” Angie teased but quickly stifled a laugh once she noticed Madison’s conflicted glance. Maybe now wasn’t the best time to start teasing.

Instead, Angie hastily added, “I’ll call Max’s teacher.”

She walked into another room while Madison settled onto the floor with the small hamster carefully positioned between her hands.

“I really like this one.”

“Me too.”

Madison watched as Max curiously peered just over her shoulder. His boyish excitement felt tangible as he tried to stop himself from bouncing around the room. He was trying his best to move slowly around the hamsters while they adjusted to their new environment.

“Why do you like this one?”

Max shrugged, "He's shy and doesn't get along with the other hamsters. This one usually sits in the corner."

Madison's heart cracked as she listened to Max. His voice sounded so sincere as he stared at the tiny ball of fluff wiggling within her palm.

"Max, how are things going at school?"

His shoulder slumped as he settled down and carefully patted the top of the tiny hamster's head. He didn't look into Madison's eyes as he sighed, "Fine. I just wish it was easier. I don't have anything cool to show off. My school projects are really good but I keep messing up when I have to talk about them."

Madison remembered what Angie had told her about Max's last school project. She knew how hard Max had worked to make everything perfect. Maybe she could offer a bit of help. It pulled on all of her heartstrings to see her best friend's kid so miserable.

"Some people are better doers and some people are better showers."

Max huffed, "What does that mean?"

"For example, I work with your mom, right? Well, I like to get my work done and let it speak for itself. Some people like to do less work and more talk. Talking is important but it's best when coupled with action."

Madison kept her gaze focused on the little fluff ball. She worried the petite creature would wiggle out of her grasp as soon as she turned away. Max grunted and sat down in front of Madison.

Perceptive brown eyes peered up in Madison's direction. He slowly narrowed his eyes and playfully wrinkled his nose.

Ever the practical kid, Max pushed, "Easy for you to say. You speak to hundreds of people on TV for a living. I would call you more of a teller. My dad says some people are a mix between doers and talkers. If that's true, I'd say that's you and my mom. Don't tell my mom I said that."

Max had a point. Maybe Madison didn't remember what it really felt like to be a kid. She remembered bits and pieces but maybe everything felt easier because she had so much life experience to use for reference.

"What's something you like to do when you're not in school? Do you like drawing or playing a sport?"

The question caught Max by surprise. His brown eyes met Madison's. His expressive face took on a comical owlish expression. He split his gaze between Madison and the little black hamster, recently named Rocko.

"Is this a trick question?"

"Nope," Madison popped the p-sound as she gently handed Rocko over. Max gently accepted the fluffy creature as it nuzzled into the bottom of his palm. A glee-filled laugh circled the room as Max stared at Rocko.

"I like to go ice skating. My dad taught me last winter. I haven't gone back since he left for his work trip to Iceland."

Madison bit her lower lip, she could tell that she needed to choose her next words carefully. She momentarily battled with herself as she struggled to determine if her next words would be an overstep. She figured that Angie would approve.

Angie always seemed to extend herself. Madison's only real friend in Lakewood was always making space for her at office get-togethers and impromptu parties. It was about time that Madison returned the kindness.

"Max, would you like to go ice skating?

"Sure, but I don't know if that will be okay with my mom. It's something that I used to do with my dad."

Madison realized the spot Max felt like he was in. He didn't want to betray his special bond with his dad by going ice skating with someone else.

"What about hockey?"

"I haven't learned how to play. All of the kids in my class know how and they all talk about going to the pond together. I sit at home when they play."

"Well, I don't know much about hockey, but I am a pretty good ice skater. How about we learn how to play hockey together?"

Max held Rocko closer to his chest as he sucked in a large gulp of air. His cheeks puffed out and he looked like what Madison imagined Rocko would look like when his mouth was stuffed with treats.

The gust of air held within Max's chest escaped with a huff. Max put Rocko on the floor. Instead of running, the tiny creature inched closer to Max's pants.

"One condition."

Madison tried to keep her cool as her mind whirled a mile a minute. What could possibly be Max's one condition? What if she couldn't agree? Would he ask for expensive hockey equipment? Madison decided she'd do her best to make it happen. Max deserved to feel proud of his hockey gear. Anything to help build his confidence. While Madison didn't remember exactly what it felt like to be a kid, she still remembered how tough it felt.

"Sure."

"You teach me how to play hockey with Mr. DeLuca. He used to be one of the best hockey players in town."

Madison blinked as she tried to imagine Vincent's father puttering around the ice. It took her a few more seconds to realize how unlikely that was. She pressed, "Are you talking about Vincent?"

Max shrugged, "I don't know. I call him Mr. DeLuca. He's very tall and he's very strong. You know he used to be the captain of the varsity hockey team. He even played in college."

Yep. Madison was glad she clarified. She felt torn between agreeing and asking for a different request. Fortunately, Max was talking about Vincent. Selfishly that meant she'd have the perfect excuse to see him again. Unfortunately, that also meant she'd need to see Vincent on the ice. When was the last time she pulled her ice skates out of retirement?

She licked her lower lip and tried, "I can talk to Mr. DeLuca and see what he thinks about the idea. But I can't promise he'll agree."

"Thank you!"

A megawatt smile crossed Max's face just as Angie returned from her call.

"What happened here?"

"Aunt Madison's going to teach me how to play hockey!"

"She is?" Angie patted the top of Max's head as she sent Madison a curious glance.

"I did," Madison tried to keep her voice upbeat as she realized the scope of her impromptu promise.

Max carefully returned Rocko to Madison's palms. He nodded at Rocko and sprinted across the room. Max wrapped his arms around his mom and cheered, "I'm finally going to fit in with the other kids. They'll want to play with me once they see I'm so good at something!"

Madison carefully returned Rocko to the cage. Her left hand absently reached up and rubbed against her heart. Max was pulling at her heart. She wanted to do everything in her power to help. What were a few face plants into the icy surface of the town's pond between friends? In the back of her mind, Madison realized she needed to start watching more hockey games. Anything to help her become the coach Max deserved. Madison also realized that she needed to make a few visits to the pond to retrace her steps before bringing Max. After a few months without practice, Madison figured she'd need a quick refresher. Madison hoped Vincent would agree to help.

"Where were you, Mom?"

"Oh," Angie's face brightened as she beamed, "I just got off the phone with Max's teacher. She'd love for you to adopt one of the baby hamsters. She said it's perfectly fine."

Madison laughed, "Thanks, Angie. I wasn't expecting such a quick response."

"I wasn't expecting to find free hockey lessons."

The two burst into laughter as Max sprinted upstairs. He wanted to show Madison his ice skates. The two women relaxed in the comfortable silence as light footsteps sprinted from one room to the other above their heads.

Tiny feet pounded down the stairs as Max returned to show off his matte black skates. He showed them to his adoring crowd and promptly put them down next to the front door.

He walked over to Madison and huffed, "Well, aren't you going to take a picture with Rocko?"

Madison noticed the confusion as it pulled at the ends of Max's brows. He folded his arms across his knit sweater and added, "My mom says it's important to take a photo when adopting an animal. Do you not take photos with your pets? That's bad. Taking photos is an important way to welcome a new family member."

Angie chimed in, "Max and I have been talking about the importance of saying versus doing. Doing acts of service and behaving in a welcoming manner go far beyond just saying the words. It's one thing to say a guest is welcome and another thing to show a guest is welcome. We're learning about the importance of saying plus doing."

Max nodded as he relayed, "Do what you say. Mean what you do."

Madison nodded and sent Angie a sharp wink. She grinned and listened to Max. He was learning a lesson that many adults well over twice his age had yet to perfect.

His sharp brown eyes looked over at Madison. Not for the first time, Madison thought Max was wiser than his years. The tilted chin and small arched brow reminded Madison of a sage little old man.

Eager to encourage the lesson, she walked over to the plush sofa in the middle of the living room. She needed to find her purse which seemed to hold everything that she needed for a day of running errands or an afternoon adopting a hamster.

"I see," Madison noted as she opened her large black purse and sifted around for her phone.

"Max, would you mind taking a picture of me and Rocko?"

Max's face brightened as he grabbed the phone and snapped a handful of photos.

"Done! See, now Rocko knows you're serious about making him part of your family."

"Good, I don't want him to feel uncertain."

A tiny squeak escaped from the cage and the trio laughed at Rocko's perfect timing. He definitely had his own little personality. Madison had a growing feeling in her chest that she was exactly where she needed to be.

Angie walked over and squeezed Madison's hand. Tears pricked at the corner of her eyes, "Thank you for agreeing to help Max."

"Don't thank me until after the lessons."

Chapter 8

A podcast dedicated to hockey techniques droned through Madison's car speakers. On the way home, she tried to repeat the names of as many hockey positions as possible. She figured that she didn't have a second to waste. A well-appointed hamster cage was safely buckled into her passenger's seat.

The drive home took a few minutes longer than normal as Madison carefully stopped and signaled at every intersection. She was afraid that Rocko would slide around in the cage if she turned too quickly. Slow and steady.

The main paved road eventually turned to gravel as Madison traveled closer to her cabin. Soaring trees blocked out the waning sun. She was sure that the call of birds and the skittering of animals would envelop the car as soon as she turned off the podcast. Small mercies. The dull voice droned on while Madison repeated every hockey term out loud.

A quaint log cabin came into view and Madison's shoulders slumped with exhaustion. She turned off the car and froze. For a minute, Madison sat in the car as she tried to piece together what was missing. She couldn't hear any animals nearby.

"Rocko, did I leave the front door open?"

The question, for obvious reasons, was rhetorical. A small puff of fur ambled from one corner of his brand-new cage to the next. Madison sucked in her lower lip and nibbled on it. Indecision made her movements stiff. She looked at the front door and paused. Her fingers toyed with her car's unlock button. One press for unlock and two presses for lock.

Lock.

Unlock.

Lock.

Double-check lock.

Madison felt stuck. She watched as the front door to her cozy cabin creaked open and closed. It swung open on the light chilly breeze, practically mocking her. She groaned. Madison tried to think of people that she could call for help. Her list started and ended with Angie. Angie was with Max so that wasn't happening. So much for that plan. She closed her eyes and desperately tried to think of a backup plan.

Her eyes carefully scanned her phone contacts. She looked at the sparse amount of names labeled with the term Lakewood. Lenny? Angie? Her boss at the news station? That would be a story.

Madison scrolled until Vincent DeLuca's name appeared on her screen. Madison wondered if she could call him. As it stood, she needed to persuade him to help Max learn how to play hockey. Madison closed her eyes as her index finger pressed the dial button.

The phone rang for several seconds and Madison decided he was busy. She was about to hang up when a masculine voice called, "DeLuca's."

Madison looked over at Rocko as he rearranged the shredded paper on the bottom of his cage. He didn't even bother to turn around. So much for moral support.

"Hi, it's Madison. We spoke at your restaurant. I also spilled coffee on you earlier in the week."

A pleased chuckle rolled from Vincent's tongue. He teased, "I know who you are, Madison. How are you?"

Madison sucked in a deep breath and weighed her options. She stared at her opened front door and started to feel silly. What if she had simply forgotten to lock it? Then again, what if she hadn't?

Before she could overthink it, she blurted, "Hi, Vincent. Are you far from the little brown cabin on the outskirts of town?"

"About five minutes away, why?"

"Well, I'm renting it and the front door is wide open."

Before Madison could continue Vincent jumped into action. She heard shuffling on the other end of the phone. "Stay outside. I'll be over in a minute."

Chapter 9

Madison hadn't expected an entire welcoming committee to show up to her quaint home in the middle of the woods, but that's exactly what happened. Two trucks barreled down her bumpy driveway and parked just a few feet away from where she was standing.

Vincent jumped out of the driver's seat and slammed the door shut. A vein near the side of his neck pulsed as he sucked in a deep breath. His shoulders only loosened once his eyes landed on Madison's sheepish figure.

He teased, "I figured we could make this a party. Madison meet the rest of the restaurant. Well, when we were running on a healthy budget."

Three men sped over and flanked Vincent. They seemed a few years older with salt and pepper hair dotting their heads. Madison coughed as she offered a small wave to the cavalry. She looked at the group and slowly got out of her car. Madison's feet crunched against the gravel as she closed the distance to the newcomers. She held Rocko's cage close to her chest. Seeing so many faces eager to help, soothed some of her earlier nerves. Now, her previous worries almost felt silly.

For some reason, Madison's thoughts kept drifting off to her cabin. Had she remembered to tidy up? Was the living room in working order? Madison mentally pushed her jumbled thoughts out of the way. She didn't have time for pleasantries. She was trying to avoid getting mangled by a possible burglar!

One of the men stepped out of the informal line and greeted, "Hi, I'm Leo.

Vincent's older cousin. He said you might be having some trouble."

Madison joked, "Maybe it's just a broken lock."

Leo sent Madison a fatherly grin as he shrugged, "Better safe than sorry. Let's check it out."

Vincent patted Leo on the back while two men who looked like perfect duplicates took the lead. Madison's curiosity got the better of her as she leaned over and whispered, "Who are the two men in front?"

"Matt and Nat. They're twins. We all grew up together."

Madison nodded as she rearranged Rocko's cage within her grasp. The metallic bars felt slippery against her sweaty palms.

"Here," Vincent reached out and carefully held Rocko's cage.

A few wayward squeaks later, Vincent held the enclosure as they entered her home. He looked at the tiny dark fluff and observed, "I didn't know you owned a hamster."

"A recent development. I had planned to get a dog, but Rocko was too adorable."

"Rocko?"

Mirth danced within Vincent's gaze as he looked between the tiny animal and Madison's reddened cheeks. He laughed, "Well, isn't that something."

"Can I tell you a secret?"

The two slowly entered the tiny cabin while the others went ahead. Madison wanted to add a bit of levity to the otherwise severe situation. A small forced smile inched along her lips as she waited for Vincent to respond.

"What?"

"I'm glad you came."

Vincent's gaze softened. He carefully placed Rocko's cage on the living room table. Vincent's voice grew a touch quieter than usual as he admitted, "I'm glad you called."

Madison looked up and held Vincent's gaze. An emotion she couldn't exactly decipher flitted across his features. As soon as it appeared, the expression vanished from sight.

Heavy footsteps bustled about in the larger lofted portion of the cabin. Leo called down the stairs, "You're going to want to see this."

Chapter 10

Ice moved through Madison's veins as her legs automatically moved up the stairs. Leo's tense tone had hinted at something out of the ordinary. Vincent's warmth seeped into Madison's back as he followed only a few inches behind. His presence bolstered Madison's nerves. Whatever lurked just out of sight, she wasn't about to face it alone.

Madison turned the corner and stumbled to a halt. Her desk was turned upside-down and her notes littered the floor. It was clear that whoever had entered her home, hadn't gotten what they were looking for. To Madison, it almost looked like someone had tossed the wooden desk onto the floor in a frenzied fit of rage.

Four men turned their cautious gazes to Madison's face. The moment felt loaded. Madison knew that her next actions would determine a new course of action. Slowly, Madison pulled her shoulders back and surveyed her bedroom. She painstakingly noted how everything else looked largely unscathed.

"That's unfortunate." Madison deadpanned as she looked around the room. The investigative part of her personality instantly snapped into action.

She pulled out her phone and snapped a few photos. Madison walked closer to the toppled desk and noticed a few wayward notes. One scrap of paper stood out from the rest. Madison plucked it from the floor and realized it wasn't hers.

Vincent instantly noticed the shift and asked, "What does it say?"

Madison stared at the sloppily written words, "Stop looking."

The room grew thick with tension. It was so quiet that the sounds of the forest easily infiltrated the room. The isolation that Madison had once loved now seemed to mock her. Maybe she was too far away from town. Too far away from any potential witnesses.

Madison closed her eyes and took a moment to collect her thoughts. Her mind moved from one piece of the ever-changing puzzle to the next. She wondered exactly what the note was talking about.

"It's not a very helpful note. I was hired to be nosy," Madison made a show of tossing the note back onto the floor. She looked at the grave faces positioned around her bedroom.

"Would anyone like some coffee? I just bought a new bag of coffee beans and made a few cookies. Well, heated up. They were prepackaged cookies. I don't know about you, but I always do my best thinking over a warm drink and a tasty bite to eat."

She snapped into hostess mode and left no room for arguments. Deep down, Madison knew she needed an excuse to leave the room. Her bedroom felt defiled. Yes, it was an overturned desk, but on another level, it was much deeper than that. Some unknown stranger had taken the time to learn about where she lived and infiltrated her private sanctuary. As a reporter, Madison felt delighted. She was on the right track for a story and a good one if her scattered notes were anything to go by.

Madison didn't wait for a reply as she headed down the stairs. She sucked in a deep breath and pulled out her coffee maker. Distant footsteps told her that the group was slowly following her lead.

Vincent looked at the miniature dining table and momentarily left the room. He returned with two more chairs easily held within his strong grip.

"I'll take a coffee with two sugars, please."

Chapter 11

The coffee pot refused to get clean. Cool water rushed over Madison's hands as she let the contraption soak. She turned her attention back to the remaining mug. Vincent stood to her right and dutifully dried off the remaining droplets. The cousins had already driven off along with the sun. A dull glow covered the kitchen as the moon made an early appearance.

Madison handed Vincent the final mug and turned off the water. She was glad for the extra company. The clinking of cups filled the compact kitchen as Vincent tidied up.

"Thanks for staying. I know it's probably a busy day for the restaurant."

"This takes priority. Besides, the restaurant hasn't seen a busy day in months."

Madison leaned against the sink and mulled over Vincent's words. She couldn't help but think that a faint thread connected the upturned desk and the restaurant drama. Madison knew the key likely rested somewhere within his words.

"How long?"

Vincent finished the dishes as his brows pulled together. He added, "What?"

"How long since the last time the restaurant had a busy day?"

The question seemed to catch Vincent by surprise. He absently scratched a hand along his sharp jawline. Madison could practically see the gears in the back of his mind churning.

"About three months ago everything seemed to stop. One accident after another. It's a shame since we put everything we could into the new kitchen. We thought it would pay off. Now it looks like the remodel is going to sink the restaurant."

Vincent shook out his shoulders and heaved out a frustrated sigh. He looked so defeated; unlike the usually upbeat man Madison had grown accustomed to seeing around town. She wanted to say something hopeful, but her words felt insincere. How could she tell Vincent that everything would be fine if it more than likely would not? She needed to find a way to help. For now, Madison felt that Vincent's face was too kind to be washed with worry. Maybe she could lift his spirit with a bit of good news.

"I still haven't told you the real reason that I called." Madison folded her arms across her chest and added, "I really wanted to ask you to play hockey."

"Hockey?"

A sparkle danced behind Vincent's eyes as he gracefully accepted the change in subject. He stood taller and prodded, "Oh? What would you like to know about hockey? You know it's not always a good idea to wait to be burgled before asking for help."

"I'll keep that in mind. I promised Angie's son that I'd help him learn how to play hockey. Max asked me to ask you. He mentioned that you used to play in high school and college."

Vincent nodded as a warm chuckle escaped his lips. The sound created a flurry of butterflies within Madison's chest once she realized just how close they were to each other. The tiny kitchen felt charged with a precarious electric energy. One false move and the current lull would snap.

Heat crept along the base of Madison's throat as she fought to look relaxed. She noticed how Vincent's gaze incrementally darkened before he cleared his throat.

"Yes, I used to play. I haven't been on the ice since the restaurant fell to pieces, but I should remember a thing or two."

"Well?"

"Well, what?"

Madison detected the teasing lilt in Vincent's voice. He wanted her to ask. Usually, Madison hated asking for favors. In fact, Madison could count on one hand the amount of times she asked for a favor since moving to Lakewood. Given what had happened earlier in the day, she was willing to make an exception.

"Will you help me teach Max how to play hockey?"

"I'm glad you asked. Yes, I can head over to the ice skating rink this Monday."

Madison clapped her hands together, "Perfect! Just one more thing."

"What?"

"Would you be willing to teach me about hockey separately? I know it's a lot to ask but I really want to know the basics."

A teasing look overtook Vincent's features as he walked over and leaned against the kitchen's door frame. He reached up and lazily gripped the top of the wooden frame. Madison's gaze wandered to Vincent's muscular arm before returning to his playful face.

If Vincent noticed her momentary appraisal, he was smart enough not to show it. Instead, he replied, "I'll do it on one condition."

"What's the condition? I might have to run it by my supervisor."

"Supervisor?"

"Yep. He's relatively new to the team. I believe you might have met him. His name is Rocko."

Vincent burst into laughter. The sound boomed around the room as the duo exchanged lighthearted banter.

"Will you have dinner with me? I want to show you a new item on the menu."

Madison tried her best to suppress the grin that threatened to overtake her face, "I'm sure Rocko will approve."

Gentle movement caught Madison's attention. She looked outside and gasped as small white flurries drifted in the evening wind. Snow landed on the forest floor and gently covered the front of her gravel-covered driveway.

"What's going on? Oh, it's finally snowing. I should go home before it starts to stick."

Madison tried to hide her dismay. Against her best effort, her shoulders tensed at the mention of Vincent's departure. Her once idyllic retreat suddenly felt unsafe. The locksmith said he wouldn't be able to come until the morning. Who knows what could happen in a handful of quiet hours?

"Unless."

Madison kept her attention glued to the window as her heart pounded in her ears. Rocko maneuvered around his cage as the first hints of the evening crept into the cabin. His movements were easy enough to track within the silence of the cabin.

"Would you like to make a few cannolis with me? I need to catch up before tomorrow."

"That's a great idea. Let me make sure Rocko has enough food and water."

"Sure," Vincent grinned as he walked over and settled into one of the plush armchairs located in the middle of the living room. He grunted and reached behind one of the pillows.

"What's that?"

Madison narrowed her eyes and inched closer. A small metallic item rested in the center of Vincent's palm. She didn't recognize it but was willing to bet that it was part of a machine.

"I don't know what that is, but I do know that it wasn't here yesterday."

Vincent wrapped the item inside of his palm "Let's get out of here."

Madison nodded as she locked the door and hopped into Vincent's truck. She noticed a few scratches around the front door's lock and groaned. She needed to replace all of her locks.

Vincent led the way as they headed out to his truck. The snow refused to stick to the ground. Madison fleetingly wondered if Vincent was right. Maybe the town was cursed.

Chapter 12

"This doesn't look right."

Madison took a step back and analyzed her handiwork. The dough appeared too liquid. Well, the word dough was generous. Her creation was closer to goo. She doubted her attempt was anywhere near close to the actual dough used to make Vincent's perfectly delectable creations.

Vincent walked over with his signature pink apron snuggly wrapped around his waist. His brows pulled together as he inspected Madison's monstrosity. He smacked his lips as he carefully looked over her workstation. His silence reminded Madison of the saying: *if you can't say anything nice then don't say anything at all.*

"How much flour did you use?"

Madison looked at the toppled measuring cups and tried to remember her previous actions. She leaned over and pointed to one of the cups as she explained, "About half of a cup."

"I see. For this recipe, we need about one and a half full cups of flour."

Madison felt mortified as she looked at her ruined dough. Maybe she could pour in the missing flour? She tossed her hands up into the air and exclaimed, "I just can't seem to get anything right."

The day's chaotic events flooded back in a rush. Madison huffed as she remembered her front door's lock was still broken thanks to a hasty burglar. So much for moving to a quiet small town.

Vincent tutted as he tried to rescue the dough. He soothed, "I wouldn't be so sure about that." Sensing Madison's train of thought, he added, "You've clearly managed to upset someone. People don't go out of their way to snoop inside other people's homes. Whatever you're looking into, just be careful."

Vincent reworked the downtrodden dough as Madison leaned against the counter and huffed, "That's easy for you to say. I don't even know what I've uncovered. So far, I've only spoken with doomed restaurants and a pet adoption agency. Pretty standard news stories if you ask me."

"Maybe you're just looking at it too closely."

Madison watched as Vincent added a little cinnamon to the dough. Her brow arched as she watched him effortlessly move around the kitchen without a measuring cup in sight. It was as if the recipes were ingrained in his muscles. After so many years, maybe making cannolis felt similar to riding a bike. Impossible to forget.

"I don't know, Vincent. All I have to show for today is a threatening letter and a random metal object."

"So you're saying you have flour and cinnamon."

"What do you mean?"

"I mean you have two key ingredients but not the entire recipe. Maybe once you know more then you'll be able to put everything together and it will make more sense."

"Maybe."

Vincent walked over and placed the dough inside the fridge to cool. He looked over at Madison and teased, "Now, we wait. Do you like sweet wines?"

"I wouldn't know. I haven't really tried too many dessert wines."

Vincent's eyes widened as he appraised Madison. For some reason, Madison felt as if she had just admitted to a heinous crime. Maybe it was practically criminal to know so little about the slower side of life. She'd been following her career for so long that she'd forgotten to make time for all of life's possibilities.

"We can change that."

****

"Are you sure this is a good idea?"

"Absolutely not. Want me to go first?"

Madison playfully shrieked as she pulled the skateboard out of Vincent's hands. She narrowed her eyes and teased, "And let you get all the credit? I don't think so."

One bottle of fruity passion wine later, the two wandered into the newly minted skate park. They had the entire park to themselves as the sun promised to rise in a mere handful of hours. The chill nipped against Madison's cheeks, but she didn't care. It was nice to do something unexpected for a change. To really live like a local.

"Wait," Vincent leaned over and strapped a helmet onto Madison's head. He playfully wiggled his brows as he teased, "Safety first."

"Sure, that's fine. I need to take a minute before doing any stunts."

Vincent arched a brow in disbelief but was smart enough not to say anything. He took a small step back and gave Madison more room.

"Thanks."

Madison sucked in a deep breath and surveyed the large skate park. Vincent's old skateboard rested under her arm as she recalled her time in New York. Madison had spent more than a few summers playing around local skate parks. While a few years had passed, she felt the distant tendrils of muscle memory yearning to come out and play. Or maybe that was the dessert wine talking?

Most of the buildings on Main Street were quiet. DeLuca's still had a few lights on in the distance. They'd probably return to the warmth of the restaurant in a few more minutes. As Madison scanned the street, she noticed bright lights turned on near the end of the street. Madison recognized the storefront as one of the local bakeries. A light moved behind the darkened window and quickly disappeared. Madison shrugged, maybe it was time for the bakers to return to their businesses.

"Do you need more than a minute?"

"What? No, I was thinking about something else. Watch this."

Madison tossed the board down and hopped on. Her feet connected and she quickly found her center of gravity. Madison careened over the top of the deck and sped over the vertical. Laughter bubbled from her lips as she found her rhythm. Madison gained speed and decided to give the quarter pipe to the left a try. She moved in an excited blur as Vincent hooted and clapped from behind.

After a few more minutes, Madison stopped a few inches away from Vincent, slightly sweaty but mostly elated. She barely registered how risky it was to try a few tricks immediately after a light dusting of snow. As Vincent had predicted, the snow hadn't stuck. Instead, the earlier white burst had already melted away.

A poorly calculated risk.

"That was amazing!"

Madison laughed as Vincent embraced her in a massive bear hug. He lifted her from the ground and playfully swung her in a circle. The two locked gazes and for a minute, it was only them. Madison blinked.

Just as soon as the moment appeared, it melted away into the past. Vincent coughed as he carefully lowered Madison to the ground and took a step back. A small smile inched along his lips as he gave Madison some space.

A cool wind whipped a few tendrils of dark hair into Madison's face. The cold returned as Vincent's warmth ebbed from her bones.

"I think the cannolis should be ready. Would you like a taste test?"

Madison grinned as she pulled her jacket closer to her body. She nodded and the two returned to DeLuca's as the sun danced along the horizon, the promise of a new day within sight.

Chapter 13

"This is Madison Crawford reporting to you live from Main Street for Channel 40 News. What you're looking at will likely be a shocking sight. As you can see, two fire trucks are currently at the scene. A fire broke out earlier and engulfed part of this well-loved local bakery. It's too soon to know the cause. The fire department will likely make an announcement later in the day. As it stands, the fire has been extinguished and is no longer a threat to other businesses on the street. We will be sure to keep viewers updated as this situation unfolds."

The lights dimmed and Madison lowered her microphone. She vaguely recognized the bakery from earlier in the morning. What were the odds that the bakery fire was caused by something that had happened during the early hours of the morning? Had she accidentally witnessed the prelude to a crime? Madison's curiosity was getting the better of her. The clock hadn't even reached nine in the morning before her boss had called and asked her to cover an emergency segment. Naturally, Madison was only too eager to jump in. Breaking news stories were few and far between in sleepy towns like Lakewood.

Charred wood and ash littered the sidewalk. Bright yellow caution tape marked off the area as onlookers congregated around the unusual sight. A soft murmur left the crowd as a few firefighters spoke with the owner.

Madison watched from a distance as she helped Lenny put the camera equipment away.

She made quick work of the task and returned to the scene of the crime. Madison knew in her gut that something was wrong. So many health code violations and unfortunate accidents didn't just happen. As a reporter, Madison refused to believe in easy answers like coincidences. What were the chances that the local restaurants would suddenly experience so many troubling problems at the same time? Madison didn't buy it for a second. Someone was sabotaging the competition.

She surveyed Main Street and counted a handful of eateries. Maybe someone wanted to keep the foot traffic created by the new skate park all to themselves. It was a shaky motive, but so far no better idea came to mind.

"Did you just cover this story?"

Madison jumped as a friendly voice conspiratorially whispered in her ear. Angie kept her eyes glued to the scene as she waited for Madison to respond.

"I thought you were picking up Max."

"I was on the way to get him from his art class but this deserved a quick pitstop. Poor Auntie's Apple Pie. This shop has been here for ages."

Madison looked at the sweet shop and winced. According to the fire department, the damage looked worse than it was. Something had caused an electrical fire in one of the outlets closest to the shop's front door. The cursive sign tilted to the side and made the once cheerful shop a pitiful sight.

"Do you know the owner?"

Angie sighed, "Who doesn't? Auntie A is famous in town for her apple cider and seasonal treats. Before you ask, no she doesn't sell apple pie. Fall is her time to shine. I'll talk to her later this week."

Madison looked over at Angie and contemplated sharing her theory. The crowd slowly departed. Once people were a safe distance away, Madison whispered, "I think this is an inside job."

"Oh?"

"There are too many coincidences. I think this could be a real mystery in the making."

Angie nodded as she took in the damaged window. "Go for it. This is your time to make a difference in Lakewood. Also, Jannie loves it when people take initiative. Treat this restaurant hunch of yours like an investigative piece of reporting. If you need any help putting this story together, let me know."

"You don't want to take this on?"

Angie harrumphed, "I'm happy with my current workload. But tell me what I can do to help you and I'll do it."

The faintest traces of a grin inched along Madison's mouth. She rubbed her fingers along her lips and tried to keep a neutral expression. Of course, Angie wouldn't be able to resist investigating. It was only natural for a reporter to feel curious.

Madison carefully eyed the crowd. They stood a few feet away from the closest straggler so she figured it was safe to whisper.

"I think someone is trying to thin out the competition."

Angie kept her face directed towards the bakery while her jaw clenched. After a moment, Angie leaned closer and asked, "Do you have any more leads?"

"No, just a feeling. Well a feeling and someone broke into my cabin a few days ago."

"What!"

So much for being subtle. Several heads whipped in their direction. A sudden lull in the crowd made it obvious where everyone's attention was temporarily directed. Angie and Madison offered their sudden crowd a sheepish wave.

Thin fingers dug into Madison's bicep as Angie pulled her friend away from the gathering. Angie ran her fingers through her long dark locks as concern covered her features.

"When were you going to tell me about this?"

Madison winced, "With a little luck, probably never."

"That's not funny."

"I know but I didn't want you to worry. It happened right after you gave me Rocko. I didn't know what to do so I called Vincent. He came over with a few men from the restaurant."

A knowing glimmer danced behind Angie's eyes as she listened to Madison. She nodded her head at the right times and made it clear that she was listening. Still, Madison had a sneaking suspicion that her friend was coming to more than a few inaccurate conclusions.

Madison hastily added, "We're just friends."

"With the most eligible bachelor in town. Good move asking for his help. Was he the perfect knight in shining armor?"

Madison rolled her eyes, "I needed to speak with him anyway. Max wants Vincent to teach him how to play hockey."

"So you asked Vincent to help you search for a burglar while also asking him to play hockey with my son?"

"Something like that."

"Did you call the police?"

"No, I didn't want to make it a big deal. At first, I thought that I had forgotten to lock the front door. I only called Vincent because my gut said that it was something else."

That same dark look returned as Angie listened to her friend. She tapped her fingers against her purse as she listened to Madison's weak explanation.

"Call the police next time. I'm sure they'd be more than happy to have a real case."

"Hopefully there is no next time."

"Are you following a lead? Yes. Then there will be a next time."

Madison grumbled, "Why is my life suddenly more exciting in a sleepy town than in bustling New York City?"

"Maybe now's your turn to shine?"

"Lucky me."

Chapter 14

Gentle sunbeams danced along the frozen pond. Madison walked over to a bench and slowly removed her shoes. She tried to flex her toes in her old skates and laughed. The stiffness of the material felt just like old times.

Young kids giggled as their parents carefully introduced them to the slippery surface. A few people stood off to the side as they watched an instructor weave between cones. Maybe Madison needed a few lessons of her own before even practicing with Vincent.

"Ready to make a lap?"

A velvety voice inquired from only a few inches away. Madison jumped in her seat. She tilted her head to the left and noticed Vincent's mirthful grin. His skates were casually laced together and slung over his shoulder.

Madison laughed, "What's with everyone in this town sneaking up on me? Yes, I'm ready to beat you as soon as you get your skates on."

"Is that a challenge?"

Madison shrugged as she watched Vincent tie his shoes. She paused for dramatic effect before she taunted, "Feels more like a promise."

The two approached the ice together. Vincent gestured for Madison to go first. She gripped the side of the wall and placed a tentative skate onto the ice. Without much fanfare, she skated to the right and turned around to wait for Vincent. Before she could pause long enough to get a proper look, a large figure glided ahead of her. Vincent coolly skated a few paces ahead. He spun around and sent Madison a cocky wink.

"I guess you'll need to learn about ice skating and hockey."

"We'll just see about that."

Madison tilted to the left as a sudden force tackled the back of her legs. A strangled yelp escaped the back of her throat seconds before her world descended into darkness.

Chapter 15

A dark bruise curved like a half-moon just below Madison's eye. She stared into the brightly lit mirror and tentatively pressed her fingers against the tender flesh. She couldn't believe a child had knocked her over. Fortunately, the kid had skated between her legs completely unscathed. Unfortunately, the same couldn't be said for Madison's face. She looked like she'd lost a boxing match. Madison stared at her newly purchased makeup kit and sighed.

"Need some help?"

Lenny hovered a few feet away from the back of the news van with a sugary donut in tow. He chomped down while he waited for Madison to reply. Powdered sugar landed on the front of his work shirt which tightly pulled against his distended belly.

"Thanks, Lenny. I'm not sure how you'll be able to make this bruised face presentable for our broadcast."

"Eh, no promises but I'm willing to give it a try. My little Elsa is a ballerina and a softball champ. I've done my fair share of stage makeup around skinned chins."

Madison arched a brow, "Your Elsa sounds like a tough kid."

Lenny chuckled, "She loves the new skate park. I'm pretty sure she'll have us take her to both the ice skating rink and the skate park as soon as she gets out of school for winter break."

Madison laughed as she listened to Lenny share about his daughter's athleticism. She could count on one hand the number of times that Lenny offered more than a few words about his personal life. The small nugget of information felt like a treasure that Madison wanted to cherish. After six months of working together, Madison was ashamed that she'd never asked him about his kids! She silently vowed to be better about managing her relationships. Mostly, that meant being more attentive to Lenny, seeing as they usually spent the majority of their shifts together.

"What do you think?"

Madison weighed her options and decided she'd let Lenny give it a go. Worst case scenario, she'd use one of the makeup wipes tucked inside of her purse.

"Thanks, Lenny. Work your magic."

Lenny nodded. He finished his treat in one bite and cleaned his hands with a wet wipe. The furrow between his brows hinted that he was taking his job as an impromptu makeup artist seriously.

"Is this your makeup kit?"

"Yep," Madison popped the last letter and watched as Lenny moved a few items around.

He grunted, "Let's see. Same idea but different tools."

"What does that mean?"

"It means I can tell you bought this from the drugstore and I think you chose a foundation two shades darker than your actual tone."

Madison's mouth opened and closed like a fish gasping for air. Never in a million years would she have expected Lenny to know a thing or two about makeup. Madison felt foolish for making such gaping assumptions about someone she worked with so closely. As a reporter, she needed to be better about avoiding assumptions.

For now, she was stuck taking all the stories that the news channel sent her way. This was the time to hone her skills. Madison knew if she stayed focused, her dream of becoming a reporter with her own news segment would eventually come true.

She didn't know what to say so she simply closed her eyes while her cameraman applied a generous layer of foundation to her face. Madison listened as he tapped away the excess makeup and used a few blotting papers.

After a few minutes, a burly voice asked, "What's with the hamster?"

Madison laughed and quickly regretted moving her mouth. The last thing that she needed was for Lenny to miss a spot because she moved.

"His name is Rocko. He's my new pet. I decided to take him on our restaurant trip. Think of him as our on-the-road supervisor."

"Will he be okay in the van?"

Madison mulled over the question. She decided that the van was definitely cool enough thanks to the moderate winter weather. The sun shone in the sky while most people donned light winter jackets.

"He should be fine. Let's just leave a window cracked, just in case."

"Why do I have a feeling that you're about to spoil this hamster like it's your only child?"

Madison laughed and Lenny grunted as her face contorted with glee. She quickly schooled her features and apologized, "Sorry, I'll try to keep from laughing. I guess you're right.

I've been so focused on work that it feels nice to pay attention to something else for a change."

Lenny added, "That's the whole point of being here."

"What is?"

"Being connected to more than our jobs. We're here to connect with each other. Fully living means agreeing to care for and witness the other people and creatures in our lives."

Madison fell silent as Lenny doused her face with setting spray. She didn't dare cough. Instead, she silently mulled over Lenny's words. What an out-of-character response. Or maybe Madison had misjudged Lenny's perceptive nature. Madison sat still and sighed through her nose. She had definitely misjudged her coworker. It was a rare moment when Madison felt pleasantly surprised after making a mistake.

"Done."

"Thanks, Lenny."

Lenny held out a mirror while Madison inspected his handiwork. Even with her poorly matched foundation, Lenny had worked his magic. Madison's makeup had never looked better.

The two stood and gathered what they needed for their upcoming news segment. Madison turned to Lenny and took in his appearance. She noticed the crinkles near the corners of his eyes from smiling too much and observed his neatly trimmed salt-and-peppered hair. Madison could really see Lenny, not her perception of him. For the first time in a long time, Madison wondered if she could really have a few close friends in Lakewood.

A silent shiver raced down her spine as they walked down Main Street. The possibility felt dampened by the feeling that she was being watched. Madison tried to reason with herself that she was a news reporter. It was only normal to have people stare while she did her job.

Madison needed a distraction. She hefted one of the bags higher onto her shoulder and asked, "Did you remember to lock the van?"

"Don't worry. Your new friend is as safe as we are."

Chapter 16

Vincent grinned as he opened the door to DeLuca's Restaurant. Madison offered him a bright smile as she helped Lenny carry some of the camera equipment into the center of the eatery.

While the restaurant looked busier than usual, it still lacked any sense of mirth. DeLuca's felt oddly dreary compared to the other festively decorated shops in the center of town.

Two tables near the front door were occupied by older patrons. A petite couple lovingly held hands as they gazed into each other's eyes. Madison gave the table a second look as she tried to remember where she had seen the duo. Given the dwindling list of eateries in town, Madison wondered if she had seen them while getting groceries.

"Your eye looks amazing. I can't believe it healed so quickly."

A bright blush inched up the column of Madison's neck. Vincent's voice carried as he walked over to greet the newcomers.

Lenny's gaze drilled into the back of Madison's head. She could practically feel his smug curiosity as he adjusted the camera equipment. After hearing so much about Lenny's personal life, Madison didn't mind him seeing a glimpse into her own private world. Not that anything she'd done with Vincent up to this point needed to be kept private.

Madison awkwardly laughed as she tucked a strand of dark hair behind her left ear. She looked up into Vincent's bright blue orbs and momentarily forgot how to breathe.

She sucked in a gulp of air and admitted, "Lenny helped me cover up the ice skating bungle. He's a jack-of-all-trades."

Vincent took a step forward and examined Madison's face. He hummed, "You're right. He covered up your freckles."

Before Madison could reply, Vincent snapped into business owner mode and offered her the newest version of the menu.

He teased, "I didn't add any of the new dishes yet. I'm hoping to get some feedback from a taste tester before that happens."

"Do you think this taste tester has a refined palette?"

"She certainly has good taste and a strong nose for trouble."

Madison's heart fluttered as she tried to remain professional. She was still at work. Besides, Madison knew that actions spoke louder than words. Vincent's eagerness to help her when she called about the mysterious break-in danced around her mind. He had dropped everything to help her. The recent scare breathed life into their tentative bond.

"The camera is ready. Want to take a practice shot?"

Madison nodded and walked over to Lenny. The moment was over. She looked around the clean but empty tables as a horrible realization settled on her shoulders. An empty restaurant didn't look good to potential diners.

"Vincent?"

"Yes?"

Madison shifted her weight from one foot to the other as she tried to tactfully phrase her concern. She bit her bottom lip and explained, "How about we highlight your new kitchen? I know it's a last-minute change but what if we do a segment showing off your homemade cannolis?"

A sparkle gleamed in Vincent's eyes as pride puffed out his chest. He nodded, "My dad loved the cannolis. It was his favorite tradition. We always made fresh cannolis before Christmas."

"Perfect. Let's bring some of that Christmas magic to the viewers at home."

"Great idea," Vincent paused.

"What?"

"Do you have a hair tie?"

"Sure. Why?"

Vincent absently scratched the back of his neck as he explained, "It's good practice to keep your hair back in a kitchen."

Madison reached up and pulled her hair into a tight ponytail. The two walked into the kitchen while Lenny followed behind.

A few minutes later, Madison felt confident she was moments away from making DeLuca's one of the most popular restaurants in town. The kitchen looked amazing. Vincent had everything arranged to show off his famous cannolis.

Vincent quietly hovered over the cannoli ingredients. His eyes stared ahead at a picture placed directly above the sink. The image showed three older men seated at a small checkered table. The youngest man struck the camera with a sharp gaze while a small child nestled into his chest.

"Who are they?"

Vincent swallowed a ball of emotion momentarily lodged in the back of his throat. He pointed to the oldest man seated closest to the camera and replied, "This is my great-grandfather. The man to his left is my grandfather. My dad loved bringing me to the family business meetings. He always joked that he taught me the family business before I could walk. My mother took the photo."

The image radiated warmth. Each person in the photo resembled Vincent. No surprise there. The dimples and soulful eyes were all clear familial traits. Madison knew she'd seen those features before.

"It's beautiful."

Vincent nodded as he sucked in a breath and confessed, "Can I tell you a secret?"

"Anytime," Madison's voice instinctively lowered a few volumes as she leaned closer to Vincent.

His lips parted as he took a moment to form the right words. He confided, "I'm camera shy."

Madison's gaze gentled as she offered, "Don't worry. You're working with a professional."

"I trust you."

Lenny announced, "About to go live!"

Madison turned to the camera as the red light switched on. A distant bell chimed as someone opened the front door. Madison kept her eyes on the camera lens as she announced, "My name is Madison Crawford and I'm reporting to you live from DeLuca's Restaurant. I'm standing with the owner of the shop, Vincent DeLuca."

Madison seamlessly slipped into the role of star reporter. The role fit her perfectly as she confidently offered the microphone to

Vincent. His face drained of color as he waved at the camera and offered an indiscernible greeting.

She pulled the microphone back to her mouth and smiled. "Vincent has kindly allowed us to take a sneak peek at DeLuca's recently renovated kitchen. Today, we are going to learn about the shop's famous cannolis. The recipe dates back over four generations of DeLucas."

Lenny panned the camera in Vincent's direction. The camera zoomed closer as Vincent stiffly piped some cream into a cannoli pastry. Alarmed screams erupted from the front of the restaurant. Madison snuck a gaze over the low counter separating the kitchen and the dining room.

The matching petite couple were on their feet as a small creature weaved beneath their table. Its small dark body scampered into the corner of the dining area.

Madison's stomach dropped into her chest once she realized what had happened. She fought to stay still. Her gaze whipped back to the camera. The smile plastered across her face never faltered. She was in her element. Internally Madison felt like hiding under a rock, but externally, she looked as calm as any other day.

"What happens after piping the pastry?"

Vincent pulled his attention away from the dining room. One of the patrons in the dining area stood up and sprinted out the front door. The bells chimed louder as if to add insult to injury.

Madison suggested, "Why don't we get a close-up to see how a true professional puts the finishing touches on a cannoli?"

Lenny zoomed in on Vincent. Madison expertly weaved out of the shot and sprinted into the dining area. She moved so quickly that she practically tripped over her own feet. Madison grabbed a to-go container and scooped Rocko into the paper contraption. She mentally whispered her apologies as she tried to contain the chaos unraveling around her.

Madison carefully placed Rocko away from the remaining diners and sped back into the kitchen just as Vincent finished adding chocolate chips to both sides of the cannoli. She inched back into sight as Lenny took a wider shot of the kitchen.

"Wow! I can't wait to try one. Come over to DeLuca's Restaurant to enjoy a tasty piece of history. I'm Madison Crawford. This has been an exclusive for Channel 40 News."

As soon as Lenny turned off the camera, Madison sunk against the kitchen counter. Her heart felt like it was about to beat out of her chest.

Vincent slowly put the cannoli back onto the counter as color steadily returned to his face. A bit of sweat dotted his brow. Madison faintly wondered if now was the right time to fess up to the rodent debacle.

Maybe she'd get lucky and Vincent would forget to ask.

"What just happened?"

Madison winced. Maybe she wasn't so lucky after all.

Chapter 17

"I can't believe it! How did the city inspectors find out so quickly? It takes them six months to fix a pothole but less than 24 hours to hear about a hamster."

Vincent shrugged, "Different city departments, I guess."

"I didn't know that made a difference," Madison huffed as she thought about how hard it was to get interviews and sound bites from city officials. Maybe Vincent was right. Maybe the health department was just more responsive?

Still, Madison's gut seemed to disagree. It felt too much like a coincidence. One thing that Madison had learned over the years was that coincidences weren't as common as people liked to think. Small coincidences usually turned out to be the hinge on which the entire investigation rested. One wayward sentence or easily overlooked detail made a massive deception fall like a house of cards in the wind.

"You left this recipe card at my house. I'm glad that I looked at it before tossing it out."

Madison tugged out the small index card and handed it to Vincent. His right brow arched in surprise as he tentatively handled the snippet of paper.

"What's wrong?"

"I don't use index cards. Most of the recipes we use at DeLuca's come from my family's secret recipe book. Where did you find this?"

"It was in the same chair you found the little metal screw. I guess this just adds to the cooking mystery."

Vincent chuckled, "Exactly. Let's see what's on this card."

Madison's throat felt dry as she pressed, "So you're saying that this isn't yours?"

FESTIVAL FAMOUS OOEY GOOEY CHRISTMAS COOKIES

4 Sticks of unsalted butter

4 Eggs

1 3/4 Cups brown sugar

1 1/2 Cups brown sugar

2 Teaspoons salt

2 Teaspoons baking soda

2 Teaspoons vanilla

4 1/4 Cups flour

4 1/2 Cups semi-sweet chocolate chips

2 1/2 Cups white chocolate chips

2 1/2 Cups dark chocolate chips

1 1/2 Cups butterscotch chips

Sprinkle sea salt

Bake at 375 degrees and keep checking after 8 minutes

"Definitely, not."

Vincent nodded as he flipped over the card and inspected the baking instructions. He added, "This is a large batch recipe."

"How can you tell?"

Vincent pointed to one of the lines near the top of the notecard, "This recipe calls for four sticks of butter. I'm willing to bet this recipe card came from one of the bakeries in town. It sounds pretty familiar."

Madison appreciated Vincent's willingness to teach her. He always kept his tone light and calm. She looked over his arm and nodded, "I just don't understand how it ended up in my house."

Vincent halfheartedly joked, "Maybe this is your first clue."

While his words were genuine, the fear deep within his gaze was unmistakable. He shifted from one foot to the other. Unease rolled between the two of them like a ship traversing troubled water.

"You don't need to worry."

Vincent's voice tightened, "See. You made it easier for me to worry. Famous last words."

"What do you mean?"

A throaty huff erupted from deep within Vincent's chest, "In horror movies, people always say last words like I'll be back or I'll be fine."

Madison teasingly rolled her eyes, "One, I don't watch horror movies. Two, we're living in real life. Besides, I like to think of my story as a rom-com or a low-stakes comforting cozy mystery. A hiccup here or there but everything turns out fine in the end"

"I think that sounds like the best option."

Madison wrinkled her nose, "Which one?"

The color in Vincent's gaze darkened as he teased, "Which one do you want to live in? Rom-com or cozy mystery?"

Energy danced just beneath Madison's skin as she ached to say something bold. She wanted to see if Vincent felt something similar. Only the final shred of sanity pulled her back from making a potentially life-altering fumble. She knew a close-knit handful of people in town. She'd be a real fool to think that Vincent's friendly actions were something more than neighborly behavior. She couldn't read too much into it, right?

The two stood in a charged silence while Max flew across the ice. His shiny neon blue helmet stood out against the seemingly endless white landscape.

Vincent shrugged as he leaned over the ice skating rink's barrier. A blue dot eagerly weaved between a handful of cones in the distance. Max hit several pucks into a miniature hockey goal while Vincent turned to the side.

After the longer-than-needed pause, Madison kept her eyes on Max while she absorbed the new information. A pit threatened to open deep within her stomach as she weighed the implications of the sudden silence. The lull in the conversation left a lingering pause.

"Will a health inspector come to DeLuca's?"

"I'm not sure. The letter mentioned health code violations."

"Health code violations?"

"Well, more like one hairy violation. Rodents on the premises."

"Let me guess. One tiny Rocko."

Madison absently rubbed the side of her temple as a headache threatened to form. Images of a little fluffy creature with terrified black eyes danced around in the back of her mind. Poor Rocko!

Vincent reached out and gently rested his palm on her shoulder. His intuitive gaze settled on Madison's worried features. Awareness washed over Madison as the respectable distance between their bodies melted to mere inches.

"It's not your fault, Maddy."

"It sure feels like it."

"Feelings might speak the truth in our heart, but they don't always listen to the knowledge in our mind."

"That's a beautiful saying. Is it from a book?"

"No. It's from a bus stop sign near Second Street."

Madison's crestfallen features lightened. The corner of her left lip twitched as it threatened to curve into a smile.

After several sleepless nights, she couldn't figure out how Rocko had escaped his cage and entered the restaurant. How had Rocko managed to scamper out of the van? What were the odds? Maybe she wasn't cut out to be a pet parent. Madison felt horrible. Rocko had ended up in a dangerous situation. To add insult to injury, Vincent's restaurant was now in trouble with the local health department. After all of the chaos, Vincent was trying to make her feel better.

"No skipping the last few cones, Max!"

A childish groan traveled across the ice as Max skated back to the start of the obstacle course. He weaved between the cones and scored a goal from about halfway across the pond.

"He's getting better."

Vincent deadpanned, "He has a good teacher."

"He does. Thanks for helping him."

"Happy to help. Speaking of helping. How is Rocko?"

The levity in Madison's chest deflated like a shiny new balloon on a hot summer's day. Madison looked down and anxiously licked her lips. They were no longer talking about Max or Rocko. It was nice to feel asked after. Usually, Angie was the only one asking. Not that Madison had given many people the opportunity to ask after her. It was oddly comforting to hear someone else checking in; even if the topic was uncomfortable.

"Rocko will be better with time. I think Rocko's convinced that discovering the truth always helps."

Vincent nodded. He looked like he was about to say something else but stopped.

Madison took it as her cue to share a secret of her own. Once Max was far enough away to be safely out of earshot, she admitted, "I feel like the robbery is the least of my worries. I can't believe Rocko managed to sneak into your restaurant."

Vincent shrugged, "I think you're onto something. Now, we just have to figure out what."

"You're right, I can't stop now. Not after getting so thoroughly tied into this mess."

An odd emotion flickered across Vincent's face. He coughed and rubbed at his chest, "Maybe it would be better if you stopped."

"Like you said, I'm already involved. I need to get to the bottom of this."

Vincent emphasized the first word of his sentence, "We need to get to the bottom of this."

“Together, we will figure this out. I have a strong gut feeling.”

“Oh? Want to share your gut feeling with the rest of the team?”

“How much longer is Max’s lesson?”

Chapter 18

The wind pressed icy flurries against cheerfully lit storefront windows. Hardened drops of water flicked across Madison's face as she precariously balanced along the side of Vincent's building. She noticed the shift in weather and tried to speed up placing the final string of lights above his storefront windows.

"Hurry up! If we're not careful, he'll see you."

Angie pulled her wool coat closer to her body. She took a few steps back and admired Madison's handiwork.

"Are you holding the ladder?"

Angie snapped back into position and held down the bottom of the ladder. She nervously laughed, "Sure. Safe as could be."

A few casual shoppers slowed their pace to take in the odd sight. It wasn't every day that people decided to put up Christmas lights right before an incoming hailstorm. According to Emily, the weather reporter from Channel 40, some of the hail was projected to measure two inches in diameter. Almost the size of golf balls. For most people, that was a reason enough to stay inside. Not for Madison.

To be fair, guilty gestures didn't always have the best timing. Madison felt awful about the health code violation. She wanted to make a grand gesture that practically screamed sorry. Madison talked it over with Angie and in less than an hour they'd managed to rustle up a ladder and multiple strings of Christmas lights. Madison stood several feet in the air as she decorated the outside of DeLuca's Restaurant.

To keep herself distracted, Madison nudged, "Max is doing great. I think he'll be ready for the Christmas Festival in no time."

Angie groaned, "I hope so. We have less than two weeks to build up his confidence. Thanks for helping him."

Madison laughed as she secured the final corner of the Christmas lights. She called down, "Don't thank me. Vincent is more than pulling his weight. Thanks to him, Max looks like a natural on the ice."

Angie laughed, "Really?"

"Yep," Madison carefully descended the ladder as a few larger bits of ice landed in her hair. She was glad that they finished decorating the window before the brunt of the hailstorm entered the town.

"Done!"

She stepped down as the rung beneath her feet broke. Madison's heart leaped into her chest as her limbs shifted away from the ladder.

Angie screamed from below as Madison scrambled for purchase. Her fingers wrapped around the side of the ladder. Madison's shoulder hissed in pain as her body swung in the air like a discarded rag doll. For once, Madison was glad she was a cheerleader in high school. Her old reflexes had unexpectedly kicked into action.

"Hold on!"

Angie's panicked voice called from below. Madison rolled her eyes as she deadpanned, "Oh, don't worry. I think I'll just hang around."

The commotion below told Madison her clumsy behavior had drawn a crowd. Great. Heat crept up the back of Madison's neck once she realized half of the town had suddenly congregated around her dangling feet.

"Don't worry, Dear! You're only a few feet away from the ground! My husband will be right back with his ladder."

The wisened voice sounded vaguely familiar. Madison craned her neck as far as she dared. She noticed Mrs. Beatie's worried face poking out of an electric yellow snow jacket about two sizes too big for her thin frame. Mrs. Beatie's husband owned Bobby's Pizzeria. The flash of recognition felt oddly comical as Madison reached up and tried to grip the ladder with her other hand. Her fingers stung as she tried to hold tight. She knew it wouldn't be the steepest fall. Still, Madison didn't want to risk a sprained ankle if she could help it.

Angie hollered, "Help is coming! Bobby brought a ladder!"

The crowd parted as Bobby stepped forward with an industrial-sized ladder. A few men from town arranged the new ladder directly next to Madison's swinging feet.

Bobby instructed, "Okay, Madison! Just stick your foot out and shift over your weight. Take your time."

"Okay! Thanks, Bobby!"

"Don't mention it. This is the most exciting thing that's happened in years."

A strangled laugh stuck in the back of Madison's throat as she unceremoniously hooked her left foot onto Bobby's ladder. Her palms burned as she shifted her hands and readjusted her weight. The crowd murmured as Madison slowly climbed down Bobby's ladder. After descending more than five ladder rungs, Madison was happy she hadn't jumped down.

Applause erupted from the crowd as soon as Madison's feet touched the sidewalk. Angie rushed over and enveloped her in a bear hug. Dark curly hair, dotted with hardened snow pressed against Madison's face.

"Never a dull moment," Angie nervously chuckled as she took the tense situation in stride.

Madison agreed, "That didn't go to plan. Thank you for helping, Bobby."

Bobby proudly patted his ladder and puffed out his chest, "Thank my wife. She told me to move the ladder into the restaurant's front storage locker, after we remodeled the to-go window."

"Glad you were around."

Eager to avoid being the center of attention, Madison looked at her handiwork and huffed. The lights weren't exactly straight, but it was close enough. A small battery pack ensured the decorations would operate without driving up Vincent's energy bill. One less headache.

A handful of stragglers looked on as the earlier commotion lulled to a dull murmur. Angie walked over to the defunct ladder while Madison took a moment to fully appreciate having her legs firmly connected to the ground. So much for manual labor.

"Hey, Madison!"

"Yes?"

Madison pulled her attention away from the four inches of lights that dipped near the "L" in Vincent's sign. Aside from the small imperfection, the rest of the lights looked great.

"Look what Bobby pointed out."

Madison stopped a few paces away from the broken ladder and huffed. The third rung from the top had broken. Madison had already figured that out from firsthand experience. She turned her gaze to the right and met Angie's troubled stare.

"Why do I have a feeling that you're not going to say something comforting?"

"Because I'm not. Look at the corner of the broken ladder rung. Do you see how straight it looks?"

"Yeah, it looks like a clean break."

"More like a clean cut. Bobby thinks someone sawed it just enough so that it would break when someone put their full weight on it."

The wind suddenly felt colder as a whirlwind of ice danced across the road and disappeared into the newly minted skate park.

"So you're saying that what happened wasn't an accident."

"I'm saying you need to be careful. What stories are you working on right now? I'll reach out to the Sheriff and see if he can be on the lookout."

A headache pulsed just behind Madison's eyes as her mind raced a mile a minute. She cupped her face and groaned as the pain in her skull ratcheted up a few degrees.

"This isn't about anything I'm covering for work. It's most likely about what I'm unofficially investigating. I guess this is a sign that I'm looking in the right direction."

"Well, look faster or you might run out of time."

"Geez, I didn't think you'd be so supportive, Angie."

Angie groaned, "I don't want to be. Clearly, whatever you've stumbled into is dangerous, but I'm not sure if whoever is threatening you will decide to stop just because you stop looking. The worst thing to be is a sitting duck."

"Angie, where did you get the ladder?"

"It belongs to Vincent. He usually leaves a few tools inside of the unlocked storage shed right behind DeLuca's."

"Do you think someone might have tried to hurt Vincent?"

Angie sent Madison a pensive stare that spoke volumes. Another burst of frigid air slashed against Madison's exposed face like a whip. It was time to go home.

Madison sighed, "I need to start narrowing down suspects. At this point, I think it's safe to say that a restaurant owner is attempting to sabotage the competition."

"I agree but who and why?"

Madison looked at Angie and tried to will an answer into existence. Who would want to get rid of the other eateries in town? What did a pizza place and a sweet shop like Auntie A's all have in common? Why would someone go through with that amount of risk? All of the most successful eateries had already suffered major blows ranging from health department woes to arson.

"Who's the most successful restaurant in town?"

Angie waved a hand in the air. She responded like the information was common knowledge. She joked, "I'll give you a wild guess." Her perfectly manicured nail pointed at DeLuca's and then indicated to Sweetie's Bakery.

"So it's a tie?"

Angie tutted, "It was before all of the health code problems started happening. DeLuca's was a popular place before the kitchen remodel. I think people forgot about it and are used to other options. But if we're talking about a classic sit-down family-run eatery, it's DeLuca's by a mile."

Maybe Vincent did have a motive after all. His restaurant still wasn't functioning at top speed. To some, that could be motive enough to want to deter the competition. Still, Madison was with Vincent when Rocko ended up in the restaurant. But then again, one of his ex-restaurant workers could have helped while Vincent was busy creating the perfect alibi. A dark thought passed through the back of Madison's mind. Was Vincent trying to throw her off his trail? After all, he had the perfect opportunity to hide the recipe card and metal screw inside of her house. Vincent might be sabotaging his place to avoid scrutiny. Wouldn't a smart culprit want to know more about the person trying to follow his tracks? While Vincent had the opportunities, Madison didn't think he had the motive. Her gut also didn't believe it for a second. Of course, Madison recognized her own emotions were probably clouding her judgment. Was she accidentally ignoring all of the clues pointing in his direction?

Madison turned her attention back to Vincent's shop. Her eyes narrowed as she tried to organize her thoughts. Madison knew one thing; something sinister was cooking. And it smelled.

Chapter 19

Hesitant eyes looked up at Madison from behind thick lashes. One small blink followed another as Max asked, "Are you sure I'll be ready for the Christmas Festival's hockey game next week?"

Vincent stood a few paces away as he took a phone call about his restaurant. His roughened voice carried over the distance and soothed Madison's frayed nerves. He'd managed to convince a city inspector to visit during regular hours. Unsurprisingly, DeLuca's passed the inspection with flying colors. Still, Madison knew Vincent felt nervous. His business was skating on thin ice after one too many setbacks. Madison wanted to ask how badly the recent closure had hurt Vincent's business. Unfortunately, she didn't know how to phrase the question. Then again, Madison already had a rough idea about the answer; it wasn't good. The added pressure from the temporary closure might be enough weight to send the entire restaurant falling through the proverbial ice.

Madison worked on the restaurant caper whenever she had the chance to squeeze in a little research between her regular news stories. Her boss, Jannie, was giving her more work than normal as they careened into the Christmas season.

Madison's thoughts returned to Max as she took in his flushed cheeks and partly unzipped puffer jacket. A light snow covered the ground. All of the locals said it would be gone before Christmas. According to the town's most famous legend, snow never sticks around for Christmas Day. It had a way of melting into the

Earth just a few hours shy of the town's biggest celebration.

For now, the light layer of snow softened Vincent's irritated voice. Madison refocused her attention on Max and attempted to keep the atmosphere light. Max was more than ready to play alongside the other kids.

"I'm not just sure, I'm positive. Max, you've worked so hard! You can score from practically anywhere on the ice."

Max tilted his head to the side as he hesitantly undid his right ice skate. His brows pinched together as he absently nodded in agreement.

That wouldn't do. Madison hadn't spent this much time and effort ice skating just for Max to leave feeling uncertain about his skills.

"How about we play a friendly game of hockey before dropping you back at your mom's house?"

"A game?"

"Yep. How about us against Vincent? First team to score a goal wins."

Max blew out a raspberry as he looked over at Vincent. Madison could tell that Max was trying to decide if playing against his coach was a good idea. A sparkle entered his eyes and he instantly perked up. Max stopped unlacing his shoe.

Madison chanced a glance at Vincent and noticed he was just about finished with his phone call. Any second now, he'd stroll back over to their conversation. She knew Vincent wouldn't be able to resist.

Mirth danced in Madison's eyes as she leaned down and whispered, "Let's give Vincent a run for his money. I'm sure he can take it."

Max nodded, "I'll say it was my idea."

Madison arched a single brow in surprise. Max sheepishly shrugged as he tried to explain, "I know how to negotiate. It's harder to say no to a kid."

"You drive a hard bargain, Kiddo."

"Not really, but I'm working on it."

Madison laughed at Max. Over the last few weeks, he'd slowly gained his confidence while navigating the ice. Each lesson helped him to stand just a little bit taller than before.

"What are we talking about?"

Vincent rejoined the group and looked between Madison and Max. His eyes narrowed as soon as he noticed the mischievous glances directed his way.

He pressed, "What did I miss?"

"Oh, nothing. Max just said he'd beat you in a friendly game of hockey."

Vincent chuckled as he took his time appraising Madison's playful glare and Max's hesitant nod. After a moment, Vincent clapped his hands together and amended, "I guess there's only one way to find out."

"Did you bring your skates?" Max looked nervous as he stared at Vincent's well-worn black snow boots. The once-white fur near the top now appeared a muted beige.

"Sure. I keep them in the truck, just in case."

"Just in case of what?"

Vincent retreated to the car as he called back, "In case you ask me to play!"

Madison smiled as she noticed Max's excitement. He quickly tied his shoe while he waited for Vincent to retrieve his skates.

"Before you ask, Vincent also has my ice skates in his trunk."

The statement might have prompted a few questions from others, but apparently, that was the perfect response for Max. He nodded his head and tapped the bench with his fingers as he waited for Vincent to return.

"What are you thinking about, Max?"

"I'm thinking about how everyone in my class will be so surprised at the Christmas Festival. After they see me play, they'll never pick me last for a game again."

Madison's chest ached for Max. She remembered bits and pieces about what it felt like to be a kid. Her school hadn't been even half as sports-oriented, so she could only imagine the type of pressure Max felt to succeed.

Before Madison could respond, Max added, "Yeah, I'm also thinking about the festival's Bake Off. We all get to vote on our favorite baked goods. The judges vote for the overall best taste, but the entire town gets to choose the crowd favorite. Last year I had like a million different desserts."

"Like a million?"

"Okay, maybe not a million but it felt like it. I had like two cookies, three brownies, and like a bunch of pie."

Madison laughed, "You're right. It does sound like you had a million different sweets to try."

"Yeah, not all of the kids could finish. The rules are that you have to try every single sweet in the competition. Mostly the bigger kids and adults make it through all of the tables."

"This Bake Off sounds like my kind of challenge."

Max laughed as he slowly got to his feet. Vincent handed Madison her skates and the two made quick work of their laces.

Vincent offered Madison his hand as they approached the pond. She gratefully accepted as she navigated the entrance to the outdoor rink.

He turned to Madison and jumped into the conversation, "The Bake Off is the best way to show off family favorite recipes. Speaking of food, I'm going to have a few people over to celebrate. Both of you should come to DeLuca's after the Christmas Festival. Max, bring your family."

A darkened curtain of emotion swept across Max's previously upbeat features. He momentarily looked down at the ice and sighed, "I don't know if my dad will be back in town by then."

"That's okay. Come over with your mom. I'll make a victory surprise to celebrate your hockey game."

Max groaned, "But you don't know if I'll win."

Vincent leveled his gaze with Max as the two leisurely skated to the center of the rink. Their blades cut against the surface. Madison's eyes tracked the spiraled patterns carved into the frozen surface.

The scene distantly reminded her of a music box that she used to play with as a child. A small ice skater with long blonde hair effortlessly spun in an elegant circle as a classical melody played in the background.

Vincent's voice held a solemn quality as he pressed, "You'll be great, Max. Remember, believing in yourself is most of the battle. Belief gets you where you need to be and practice takes you the rest of the way."

An uncertain voice conceded, "Okay, DeLuca's sounds like fun."

"That's the spirit. Now that we're all on the ice, what are we going to play?"

"The first team that makes a goal wins?"

Vincent chuckled, "May the best team win."

He pulled out a puck from the front of his snow jacket. Vincent gently tossed the smooth dark object into Max's palms.

Madison asked, "What are we playing for?"

Max hollered from a few feet away, "We're playing for bragging rights and cookies!"

Madison and Vincent echoed, "Cookies?"

"The winner gets cookies."

Madison laughed, "Well, bragging rights and cookies are enough to motivate me. Let's play!"

A gruff voice agreed, "I could get used to that."

Madison looked at the group and pressed, "Let's memorialize this bet before anyone wins."

"How do you suggest we do that?"

Madison laughed as she fished her phone out of the front pocket of her winter jacket. She held it out and grinned.

Vincent chuckled, "Since when did you start taking so many photos?"

"I'm not sure, but it feels right."

"Want me to take our photo? I might have a better angle."

Madison laughed, "Go for it. Between the two of us, it's no surprise that you have the larger wingspan."

"Are you calling me a bird?"

"No, I'm just calling you tall."

Vincent carefully took Madison's phone and positioned their faces in the center of the screen.

"Not exactly an amazing compliment, but I'll take it."

"You will?"

"Yep."

"How do you know I mean it as a compliment?"

Vincent chuckled, "I'm willing to give you the benefit of the doubt. Also, famous DeLuca pride, remember? I can't see it any other way."

"Very funny. Don't worry, I mean it as a compliment. We're exactly a foot different in height."

"I thought it was more."

"Don't push it, Mr. Wingspan. Otherwise, I will call you a bird."

"You're right. My pride definitely can't take that."

Madison grinned and inched closer to Vincent. The action felt friendly enough as she tried to keep a respectful distance between their bodies.

Vincent was so close to Madison that his warmth seeped into her body. His shoulder gently brushed against her side as the two leisurely skated closer to Max. Blood rushed through Madison's veins as a thrill raced through her body. She took her phone back and the two skated in Max's direction. Vincent held out his outstretched palm and nudged it near Madison's hand.

For a moment, Madison contemplated ignoring the gesture. What if he was simply stretching his hand? What if she misread the gesture and it ruined the entire friendship? Worst of all, what if she overthought everything and ruined her own chance at happiness? The last question struck her the hardest.

Madison reached out and intertwined her slim fingers with Vincent's calloused digits. He gently clasped his much larger hand over Madison's. The two skated ahead in perfect unison without saying a word.

Max looked between the two adults and shouted, "Are you two ready? Let's play!"

Chapter 20

The Christmas Festival appeared as quickly as a motivated hockey player moving across the pond. In less time than Madison had thought, the festival that she had heard so much about finally arrived. The flyers posted around town promised exciting games, rides, prizes, competitions, and of course, hockey.

The school-backed hockey games seemed to be all Lakewood could talk about. Whenever Madison ended up behind someone in the grocery store, the conversation circled back to the impending age-ranked skirmishes. Given the size of the tight-knit community, the school taught students from kindergarten all the way up to eighth grade. Each grade level competed for ultimate bragging rights. Understandably, the eighth graders and seventh graders tended to come out on top for the annual school-wide hockey trophy. Still, people around town liked to bring up unexpected wins like last year when the second graders managed to beat out the fourth graders.

Madison walked over to her bathroom mirror and took extra care fixing her dark locks. She felt out of practice when it came to achieving a relaxed look. Her makeup routine for work was quickly tossed to the wayside in favor of a more natural look. When broadcasting, Madison needed to pack on the foundation to ensure the camera picked up her image. Since she started working with the local news channel, she typically went through foundation like water. It felt nice to be able to have a day off. Madison applied a thin layer of tinted chapstick to her lips. She scrunched the front of her dark hair and noticed how the loose waves framed her angular face.

"It's time to get this show on the road," Madison turned to Rocko and laughed. His rotund body shook with every step he took while running on his circular wheel.

Rocko's presence added joy to her forest-hugged house. Madison snapped a picture as Rocko moved around his enclosure. The movement made the image look blurry around the edges but Madison didn't care. The photos on her phone were slowly telling the story of her life. A life filled with more mysteries and adventures with every passing day.

As far as pet parents went, she still wasn't the best. How had Rocko managed to get into Vincent's restaurant? The unanswered question constantly danced a jig in the back of Madison's mind. For some reason, her gut told her that a few answers were right around the corner. She just worried about what else lurked behind the bend…

Chapter 21

Children screamed with glee as they sprinted around the designated festival grounds. Madison had never seen anything like it in her life. Decorated storefronts hugged the jovial crowd. Countless strands of holiday lights and ornament-laden garlands wrapped around Main Street's storefronts. The celebration stretched from the center of the street and extended all the way to the closest fully frozen pond. A sign proudly encouraged townspeople to visit the new skate park between hockey games.

"Excuse me!"

Tiny pigtails brushed against the side of Madison's jeans as she awkwardly stumbled over the uneven curb. The petite child looked familiar as she confidently moved around Madison like a surly billy goat ascending a mountain.

A flurry of warmly bundled kids sprinted over to the food stands near the newly constructed skate park. Madison could hardly believe how active the kids were. They effortlessly bounced from one sport to the next. The grade schoolers balanced on their skateboards and careened down ramps while patiently waiting for their turn to battle it out on the ice rink.

"You knocked into that old lady!"

The little girl with pigtails shouted back, "I said excuse me!"

Each excited holler blended into the next as the group collectively fled into the safety of their childhood stronghold. Madison opened and closed her mouth as she processed the comment. Old? Who were those little squeaks calling old? After a minute, a surprised laugh escaped her lips and floated along the energized breeze.

She realized why the little girl with pigtails looked so familiar. The little fireball was Lenny's daughter.

"What have you in such good spirits?"

"The Christmas spirit?"

Vincent laughed as he handed Madison a cup of steaming cider. He shook his head, "That was cheesy."

He smelled of fresh pine needles and smoke. A thin layer of stubble covered his strong jaw. He took a sip from the steaming cup. Madison realized Vincent hadn't slept.

She gratefully accepted the festive beverage and took a sip.

"Thank you. It's delicious. Where did you get this from?"

Vincent gestured to the food stands placed near the outskirts of the skate park. A cursive sign hung in the distance.

He pointed, "Auntie's Apple Store."

Madison snorted, "You're kidding."

"No, it's a store on the opposite end of Main Street. Look." Vincent pointed across the street to a tiny store with a slanted sign and a burnt storefront.

Madison hummed as something about the sight demanded her attention. She crossed the street and stopped a few paces away from the downtrodden sign. Vincent easily kept pace.

"Are we looking for clues?"

"Yes. Do you still have the small metal piece we found in my cabin?"

Vincent dug around in his pocket and pulled out the screw. He looked at the slanted sign and whistled.

"Your intuition is impressive. The screw looks like a perfect match."

"Thanks, can you fix the sign?"

Vincent laughed as he pulled out a small screwdriver from his pocket and admitted, "Way ahead of you. Can you hold the drinks?"

People gave Vincent curious glances but didn't stop him from fixing the sign. Some townspeople even called his name as they walked in the opposite direction.

"Done. I can't believe you recognized the screw. Not even five minutes into the festival and we've already solved a mystery."

Madison laughed, "Sure, but I'm hoping for a little more excitement than replacing a missing screw. Do you think I could talk to Aunty A?" She took a small sip of her drink and soaked in the sights.

Vincent nodded, "Sure, she looks a little busy with customers but I'm sure she won't mind."

Madison followed his gesture and noticed how the line within the makeshift food court for Aunt A's stretched several feet. She needed to be thorough.

"Let's go."

Vincent nodded as he led the way over to Auntie A's. They waited in line with their ciders still in tow. A sweet older woman with reddened cheeks and bright orange hair grinned.

Auntie A pointed at the cups and teased, "They're not even empty yet."

Madison switched into investigative mode. She greeted, "The cider tastes delicious. My name is Madison. I'm from Channel 40 News. I covered the story of your bakery earlier in the month. I'm glad to see you."

"Oh! That's right! I remember you. It really is a shame. The fire department still doesn't know how that happened. They think it might have been caused by negligence but my staff is always so careful about these things. I'm hoping the funds from the festival will be enough to fix the damages."

Madison frowned, "So your insurance won't cover it?"

"Not unless someone can prove it was arson or faulty wiring."

Auntie A's weathered face looked troubled. Madison chanced a glance at the quickly building line and shifted the conversation. She doubted the mastermind of the local restaurant blues came from the sweetest old lady in town. Auntie A didn't have a reason to burn down part of her own store.

"Thanks for talking with us. We'll let you get back to your customers. If we find anything out, we'll let you know."

Auntie A waved goodbye as Madison and Vincent retreated from the stand. Madison organized her thoughts as she processed the new information. She sucked in a deep breath and released it in a huff.

"I can't believe a town like this exists. It's so special to see everyone come together and celebrate."

"Consider this event your belated gift from the welcoming committee."

"The most thoughtful welcoming committee that a girl could ask for."

Foot traffic commanded the entirety of Main Street. Lights glimmered in the distance. A green and red Ferris wheel stood in the center of the road. The line for the famous ride looked promising. A lone couple embraced near the front of the Ferris wheel's barricade while most festival attendees congregated near the food stands and skate park. Madison stared at the ride and grinned. That was definitely on her list of things to do during the festival.

"Want to go on the Ferris wheel?"

"Am I that transparent?"

Vincent winked, "Plastic wrap."

"Fine, if I'm so easy to read, what do I want to do first?"

Madison tried to keep a straight face. What were the chances that he'd say that she wanted to walk around with the cider before hopping on the Ferris wheel? Close to zero. She liked her odds.

"Let's look at the food stands and then come back to the Ferris wheel."

Her odds were horrible.

"Have you considered moonlighting as a psychic?"

Vincent choked down a sip of his cider. He shook his head and led Madison to the food stands. Townspeople packed into the grassy area while Christmas songs played from a few speakers placed near the outskirts of the makeshift food court.

"I don't even recognize half of these faces," Madison moaned. She took a sip of her drink and embraced the warmth that raced down the back of her throat.

"That makes sense."

Madison jumped in, "I know. I haven't made much of an effort to put down roots. It wasn't until last week that I realized that Bobby is married to Mrs. Beatie."

"Mrs. and Mr. Beatie are the unofficial leaders of this town. They're always offering to help. You're putting down more roots than you give yourself credit."

"It doesn't feel like it," Madison looked around the tented area and frowned. The condensed food selection fought with the image Madison created in her head. Max had talked so much about the food that the sparse selection of eateries somehow felt lacking.

After a beat, Madison couldn't keep her curiosity away. The words burst from her mouth like water from a poorly built dam. "I thought there'd be more tents or stalls or well, more something."

A dark look crossed Vincent's features. He tried to keep his composure, but Madison saw right through him. He couldn't hide the pinched muscles near the corner of his jaw.

"What?"

Vincent kept his gaze directed at something in the distance. Madison followed his stare and found nothing of importance. A few teens stood in an ever-growing line for powdered strudel while they cracked confetti eggs over the top of their friend's heads. Brightly colored pieces of paper fluttered onto the white-flecked grass. It was hard to believe that the snow would disappear before Christmas. Well, at least according to legend. But then again, town legends seemed to be rewritten daily. The story about the endless food stands? Madison counted less than ten pop-up stalls. Hungry customers stood in winding lines, eager to indulge in more filling festival fare.

"I thought there would be more food stands. Max made it seem like this area would be packed."

Vincent rubbed the back of his neck with his palm as his guarded blue eyes carefully assessed the crowd. After a moment, a sigh passed his lips, "Usually it's one food tent after another. Things change."

"What's changed?"

Madison had a hunch she knew at least some of what had changed but she wanted Vincent to confirm her suspicions. She didn't want to ask any leading questions when she finally felt so close to the truth. Madison wanted to hear it from him. No, she needed Vincent to confirm her suspicions.

"I'm usually working the Christmas Festival. You see that empty spot next to the coffee tent?"

Madison nodded.

"That's where DeLuca's Restaurant used to sell the best homemade cannolis. We would prepare several days in advance. The cannolis were a real crowd-pleaser. We used green and red sprinkles at the ends of each pastry."

Vincent's eyes watered as his lower lip disappeared between his teeth. He chanced a glance in Madison's direction and winced, "I'm ruining the festive mood."

"You don't need to apologize for having feelings. I feel bad because part of this mess is my fault."

"It's not your fault, Mads. DeLuca's was in trouble months before Rocko paid it a surprise visit. You met my cousins. I haven't been able to employ them in ages. Without the extra hands, I couldn't make enough cannolis for this year's festival. After all this time, I'm starting to think that maybe it's just a sign."

"A sign of what?"

Madison finished her cider and waited for Vincent to respond. His eyes were so expressive that a few glances conveyed everything he wanted to say but couldn't fully put into words.

He tried to lighten the mood, "I guess this is what makes you such a good reporter. You see everything. Come over to DeLuca's after the festival. I prepared a celebratory dinner."

"Don't worry, I'm planning on being there bright and early."

"Why? Does the front window need more Christmas lights?"

Madison covered her face and sighed, "Who told you?"

"It's hard to keep a secret when half of the town sees you dangling off a ladder in the middle of Main Street."

The duo passed a line stretching well into the center of the makeshift food court. Sweetie's Bakery stand offered delicious cookies and a few festive cupcakes that looked like a true customer favorite. Across the way, one stand had a less-than-eager crowd. Adding insult to injury, the trashcan closest to the mostly ignored tent overflowed with half-eaten baked goods. Behind the counter, a thin man with stormy eyes looked understandably grumpy. Madison theorized he was probably the owner.

She nudged Vincent, "Who is that?"

"Oh, he owns the newest bakery in town. He really is a piece of work."

"What makes you say that?"

"I went over to his bakery when it first opened. He acted like I wasn't there as soon as I told him about DeLuca's. It wasn't a great first impression."

Madison knew whatever had happened was likely worse than Vincent was letting on. He wasn't the type to gossip. Madison let the topic drop but made a mental note to look more closely into the newcomer once the festival came to a close.

Vincent leisurely led them away from the food court and looped back to the Ferris wheel. The couple from earlier swung several feet above the ground in a spacious green seat.

A young kid in his early teens opened the ride's gate and helped them board. Vincent's thigh brushed against Madison's as he settled into the large metallic seat. While Madison's feet were a few inches off the ground, Vincent's easily touched. Their height difference looked almost comical if a passerby only glanced at their legs.

Maison nodded at the teen, "Thank you."

A crackly voice answered, "Don't mention it."

The lap bar clinked safely shut and the seat lifted into the sky so more riders could join.

"The seat's pretty large," Madison noted. The edge of the metal nudged against the back of her calf and awkwardly pressed her leg into an upward position. She felt like a kid sitting at the grown-up's table.

"Yeah, maybe this ride was designed for giants," Vincent stretched his arm and rested it over the back of the seat. He kept his eyes on

Madison's face and carefully gauged her reaction.

Madison flashed him a reassuring smile. His hand ventured closer and lightly landed behind her shoulders. The breeze carried the scent of apple cider and freshly baked cookies as the two crept higher into the sky.

The Ferris wheel stopped and Madison realized they could see the entire town from the top of the ride. Her breath clogged in the back of her throat as she took in the view. Children sprinted through the festival grounds while parents chatted around a few collapsible tables. The community ebbed and flowed in waves as people circulated the festival grounds.

"It's beautiful."

"I know."

For a moment, Madison had a fleeting idea that Vincent wasn't just talking about the view. She stared out at the sea of movement below and smiled. Madison wondered what the festival would look like next year. She stopped mid-thought. Next year? Was she already planning to put down deeper roots? It wouldn't be the worst thing in the world to live somewhere where your neighbors actually knew your name and your coworkers asked to come over for dinner.

"What are you thinking?"

Energy crackled between them as Madison leaned back against Vincent's arm. She inhaled the scent of his woodsy cologne and inched closer.

So close.

Madison closed her eyes and leaned forward. She wanted to end the tenuous game of cat and mouse that she'd been playing with

Vincent for so many weeks. At first, it was so subtle that she hadn't been sure that Vincent felt it too. Now? She didn't need another clue.

The Ferris wheel jolted into action a moment before their lips touched. The abrupt movement pushed Madison against Vincent's warm firm chest.

She blinked. In the span of that moment, everything and nothing had somehow managed to change.

Chapter 22

"Let's go, Max!"

The halftime ended in a roar. Horns blew as students cheered for their schoolmates. The third graders easily kept pace with the fourth graders. Parents clapped from the elevated stands while a few people pressed against the ice rink's barrier for an up-close view of the action.

While Madison cheered Max on, she noticed how much smaller he was compared to his classmates. In some ways, Madison realized his slight size worked in his favor. Max zipped along the ice and easily outmaneuvered the other kids. He deftly controlled the puck while skating around kids from the opposite team.

Madison leaned against the waist-level barrier and hooted. Angie stood to her left while Vincent hovered close to her side. The game was close.

The crowd went wild as the kids attempted to break the tie. It was more exciting than any game that Madison had watched on television. To be fair, she wasn't much of a television watcher. During her days off, Madison preferred to thumb through the mystery novels stacked near her fireplace. She couldn't remember the last time that she had sat down and turned on the small TV in her cozy cabin. Come to think of it, Madison wasn't even sure if the remote in her cabin had batteries.

Maybe she was finally so busy living her own life that she didn't have time to indulge in the lives of fictional people.

Books didn't count.
Obviously.

One of the bigger kids in Max's class sprinted across the ice and lobbed the puck in Max's direction. The puck gained air and sped towards the front of Max's shirt.

Instinctively, Madison cupped her hands around her mouth and shouted, "Get it, Max!"

Max shifted out of his frozen position and stopped the puck. The puck landed on the ice and Max wasted no time passing it to another kid. His skills were so good that Madison almost forgot he had picked up the sport in less than a month. She loved seeing his confidence as he took control of the rink. Even a few fourth graders moved out of the way once they noticed him approaching.

"Unbelievable."

Angie leaned to the side and gushed, "He's a fast learner just like his father."

Madison's lips thinned as she watched Max. He was in his element. It was too bad his father wasn't able to watch his newfound success. Madison couldn't imagine the tradeoffs Angie and her husband needed to navigate between raising Max and maintaining careers.

She tilted her head in Angie's direction and asked, "By the way, where is he?"

Angie sighed, "Hugh said he'd try to make it, but the weather has been so bad in Reykjavík. All flights have been grounded for the foreseeable future. Hopefully, he'll be home before Christmas Eve."

The pinched nerve between Angie's brows hurt Madison's heart. She felt deeply for her friend. Although she'd only heard about her friend's husband, Madison felt like she already knew him.

"Let's take a few photos and videos to remember the game," Madison suggested. She held up her phone and leaned against Angie. Kids popped in and out of the background of the frame as they sped around the ice.

"Here. Let me," Vincent held out his hand and Madison gratefully accepted his offer.

"Thanks."

Angie teased, "Oh, look who's suggesting we take photos now."

Madison playfully rolled her eyes, "People change."

Angie corrected, "People grow when they're ready."

Madison opened her mouth to offer a smart retort. Instead, Vincent instructed, "Say hockey."

Angie and Madison cheered, "Hockey!"

"Let's see what the photos look like."

Madison laughed, "I'm sure they look great."

A cheer erupted from the crowd as one of the fourth grade girls swooped in and grabbed the puck. Her mischievous giggle twinkled like chimes as she slid between two kids. Madison couldn't help but notice Max's intent stare. His eyes held a starstruck quality as he watched the young girl with two long pigtails fearlessly navigate the ice. Max was looking at the little girl who had called Madison an old lady. Lenny's daughter, no less. Maybe Max had more than one reason to learn how to play hockey.

It seemed the more that Madison learned about the dynamics of a small town, the less she really understood. There was always something else just outside of the frame, prepared to add another layer to the story.

"What's so funny?" Angie looked over Madison's shoulder and stared at the photos taken on the phone. She inspected the images for anything out of the ordinary.

"Nothing. The photos are perfect," Madison handed her phone over so Angie could have a better look. It wasn't her place to tattle on what she suspected was a little crush.

The clock above the scoreboard counted down the last ten minutes of the game. With the grades tied, it was possible for anyone to snag the bragging rights and move on to playing the fifth graders.

"Excuse me, sorry. Have you seen my wife?"

A kind-eyed man in a snappy tan suit walked through the crowd. His strong posture and confident stride told Madison everything that she needed to know. Angie's husband had pulled off his own version of a Christmas miracle.

"Honey!"

Angie wrapped her arms around the back of her husband's neck. The couple embraced and eventually pulled away. Angie's husband kept one of his hands gently pressed against the back of her wool coat. Madison attempted to offer the duo some semblance of privacy by looking in the opposite direction. For some reason, their fond embrace held an elevated level of intimacy. Perhaps because their eyes spoke words that the random passerby couldn't understand. Madison wondered what it would feel like to have someone in her life that she wanted to share her days with. Maybe even share her lazy mornings on her rare but deeply cherished days off.

"What's the score?"

"It's tied," Madison smiled as she met her best friend's husband.

"You must be Madison. It's great to meet you. My name is Hugh. I am ashamed it's taken us this long to finally get acquainted. Work was busier than usual this season."

Madison waved her hand in the air. She grinned, "It's okay. Always better late than never."

Vincent clapped Hugh's back. He laughed, "Welcome back to town. Any longer and we were going to send out a rescue party."

"Much appreciated. I took the first plane out as soon as the weather eased. What did I miss?"

"One goal per team."

Madison listened to the playful banter as the group reconnected. She leaned closer to Vincent's side. It felt nice to be in the presence of a human furnace.

"Go, Max!"

Four heads whipped over to the ice just as Max sped down the center of the rink. He dodged a few kids and faked out a handful more.

"Max!"

The cheer rumbled across the ice as Max scored the winning goal. A chime resounded from the top of the scoreboard. The game was over.

Max turned in the direction of the stands. He scanned the crowd pressed against the barrier and waved.

"Did you see me, dad?"

"I sure did, Pal!"

Vincent leaned down and whispered against the shell of Madison's ear. His minty breath fanned the side of her face, "Do you know what that means?"

"I have a feeling you're going to tell me."

A deep chuckle rumbled out from the back of Vincent's chest, "It means I owe Max a feast."

Madison teased, "I've never loved that kid more."

Chapter 23

"I don't think I've ever been more excited about winning a hockey game."

Vincent laughed, "Same and I've played with some pretty intense competition."

"You never played against a fourth grade team."

"You're right. Max has me beat. He even played against the fifth graders."

Madison laughed, "Now that was a sight! I couldn't believe the height difference between the third graders and the fifth graders."

"It's a shame the fifth graders won."

Madison grinned as they walked around the rest of the festival. She joked, "Max will get them next year. Just imagine how good he will be in another year."

Bake Off stalls curved around the left side of Main Street. Madison counted over 20 different stalls before giving up. How was it possible that there were more contestants in the baking competition than all of the regular food stands combined? Madison hadn't thought there would be such an obvious gap.

"The competition for best baker looks pretty stiff."

Vincent carefully appraised the tables and hummed. His noncommittal answer stoked the flames of Madison's curiosity.

She groaned, "Don't tell me. There used to be more stalls."

"Do you see that lamp post on the opposite end of the street?"

Vincent pointed into the distance and Madison squinted. At first, she missed the lamp post because it was so far away. She nodded,

"Are you teasing me because I don't know any better?"

"Honest, Mads. I can show you photos. Usually, this competition fills up the center of Main Street. People used to come from three towns over to show off their skills."

"What do you think changed their minds?"

"Maybe they didn't want to end up ruined like half of the restaurants on Main Street."

Madison looked around and realized Vincent was right. For every open restaurant on Main Street, another seemed permanently shuttered or at least well on its way. While the decorations surrounding the storefronts masked the dire situation from a cursory glance, the festivities did nothing to hide the truth from a discerning eye.

"Wow. I had no idea it was so bad."

"We're a small town. Even one family-owned restaurant is a loss. More than three? It's a tragedy. I can't blame the bakers from out of town for wanting to avoid our bad luck. Who knows if it's contagious."

Vincent's joke fell flat. Without thinking, Madison reached out and held Vincent's hand. She offered her support as she fully took in the gravity of the situation. It was impossible to ignore with such a stark visual right in front of her face. The darkened storefronts and missing booths were a harsh reminder of the mystery Madison knew she was on the brink of solving. She was so close.

Madison felt like she was looking at the clues like different parts of a recipe. At this point, she was just missing the secret ingredient.

Madison closed her eyes and thought back to Rocko scampering around DeLuca's. She tried to temper her excitement as she asked, "Do you have a camera in DeLuca's?"

Bingo.

"Yes, but it's pointed away from the front door."

A small grin worked along the edges of Madison's blue lips. The temperature felt like it had dropped ten degrees since the start of the celebration. The possibility of catching the culprit ignited a fire in her belly.

"Want to share the tapes with me after dinner?"

Vincent playfully teased, "That depends."

"On what?"

"On how well you handle this bakery Bake Off challenge."

The two walked over to a man in a cartoonish top hat offering pink tickets to serious eaters. He shared with them the rules of the Bake Off and advised them to pace themselves.

Madison accepted the Bake Off tickets and miniature pencils provided so they could write down their favorite bakers. She turned back to Vincent and handed him his own ticket and pencil.

"I don't know if I have the right stomach for this challenge. I counted about 20 different stalls before giving up."

"Don't worry, all of the desserts are miniature. I think it would be too dangerous to try and eat over 20 full-sized desserts before the end of the day."

Madison added, "Well at least that's the kind of danger that I can get behind."

"Not me. I'd be sick for days."

Madison laughed, "Same here. I just don't think I would regret it. Or maybe I would regret it, but that wouldn't stop me from doing it again next year."

"Lucky for you, this Bake Off was designed to be challenging but not impossible. It's probably one of the few competitions where both the judges and the contestants really need to put in the work."

Madison nodded as her eyes scanned the various tables. She hummed in the back of her throat. "Do you think someone made apple pie?"

"It's possible. Why?"

"Apple pie is my favorite but I rarely get the chance to eat it. My mom used to make an amazing apple pie. She still does, but I no longer live close enough to grab a bite. Making an apple pie for someone else is the best way to say I love you. It's time-consuming but so worth it in the end."

A comfortable break in the conversation settled between them as they leisurely inspected the stalls. They wandered down Main Street while casually getting a lay of the land. Madison could hardly believe it. She'd counted over 30 different contestant stalls. More than double the amount of restaurants in all of Lakewood.

Curiosity bubbled in the pit of Madison's stomach as she took in her surroundings. The investigative part of her recognized how perfect it would be for someone to sabotage the competition. If a restaurant ruiner was around, surely this was the perfect opportunity to create chaos. Or was it?

Chapter 24

"What are we looking for, detective?"

"Very funny," Madison glanced at Vincent from the corner of her eye. She didn't want to look suspicious as they circled the baking competition.

They were about halfway through tasting all of the delicious confections. Even with miniature tasting samples, Madison was well on her way to getting stuffed. Her belly reminded her of the snowman that the kids in the center of the skate park were diligently rolling with the remaining snow. The misshapen snowman was a sight that would make Picasso proud. A smirk inched its way along Madison's lips as she noticed a second snowman being built only a few feet away from the first. Even with a mystery afoot, Madison found herself distracted by their childish antics. Spending so much time with Max was making her think. Maybe a white picket-fenced yard where Rocko could zoom to his heart's content wouldn't be so bad. In the distant future, of course.

"Where did you go?"

Vincent pulled Madison away from her runaway train of thought. A light blush crawled up the sides of her neck once she realized she'd been caught. Unwilling to lie but also unwilling to admit that children building snowmen had pulled at her own desire for a family, she settled on a joke.

"The kids are making snowmen capable of defying gravity."

"It's a miracle."

"Not yet, the real miracle would be if the kids were able to make a snowman on Christmas Day."

Vincent teased, "See, now you're speaking like a local. Who knows, maybe this will be the year we break the curse?"

"What makes you say that?"

"I'm feeling lucky."

Madison stared deep into his soulful blue eyes. For the second time in less than 24 hours, Madison considered kissing him. Would that count as a calculated risk? She wasn't sure. Instead, Madison redirected her attention to what she did know. The restaurant ruiner was somewhere in this jovial crowd. Madison's gut knew that they were going to strike again.

After what felt like another endless round of sweets, Madison finally sampled the last contestant's delicious pumpkin pie.

"Can I tell you a secret?"

Vincent leaned down, "Anything."

"I still want apple pie."

Vincent's ears perked up as he parroted, "You do?"

"It's my favorite dessert. Nothing fixes a bad day like a delicious apple pie."

"Noted."

Madison pulled out her ticket and awkwardly wrote down her top choice while using the side of a tree as a makeshift desk. She thought it was a pretty tough competition but ultimately some chocolate cookies managed to win her over. The cookies were pure gooey richness thanks to a generous helping of various chips which made every bite even better than the last. The baker appeared to be a vaguely familiar woman in her late 20s. Madison wondered if she'd run into her before.

"What are some of the most important things to have when setting up for the Bake Off?"

Vincent stared down the expansive line of tables. His brows furrowed in concentration as he inspected the contestants for even the slightest dissimilarity.

"Most of the work happens before even coming to the competition. The treats come pre-made. Most of the bakers probably stayed up late to make sure their samples were ready for the morning. Maybe refrigeration or storage. Having enough plates for the samples is also important."

"I see."

Madison felt stumped. How could someone ruin a competition where everyone cooked their treats separately? It felt unlikely that someone could sabotage all of the different kitchens within the span of a night.

A voice called over the speaker, "We are about half an hour away from announcing this year's Bake Off champion. Please head over to the front table to turn in your pink tickets. Don't forget to write in your favorite baker on the back of your ticket."

Bodies flowed down the street and pressed closer to the Bake Off's ticket table like a wave crashing against the shore. People quickly handed their tickets over to the man in a top hat. Madison's gaze traveled over the crowd before it snapped back to the man behind the table. His build looked a good 30 pounds slimmer than before.

Wait.

"Vincent, does the man at the ticket table look a little thinner than before?"

Vincent grunted, "Yeah. Let's go turn in our tickets. Are you ready?"

"I just wrote it down."

"Let's go," Vincent reached down and led Madison through the crowd. His height made it easy for him to clear a path.

He beelined for the front table where a distinctly different person quickly collected everyone's pink tickets. Madison frowned, the man donned a fake beard and a top hat so that he vaguely resembled Abraham Lincoln. It was a far cry from the original ticket collector's jovial carnival-inspired appearance.

Vincent swiftly moved through the crowd. His broad shoulders and familiar face worked wonders as they navigated the throng.

"Tickets?"

A vaguely familiar face looked up at Madison. The man's mouth moved over the word like molasses. His eyes widened as he took a step back.

Madison knew. Her gut knew something was wrong and his actions quickly confirmed her suspicions.

"Hey! Who are you?"

The bag of collected tickets fluttered to the ground. Vincent tried to get to the man but the crowd swallowed the stranger whole. An Abraham-inspired top hat rolled along the ground while its recent wearer was nowhere to be found.

Madison spun in a circle. She couldn't believe it. Another ploy had almost happened right under their noses. Deflated, Madison walked around the table and joined Vincent in the center of the ticket-returning crowd. One thing was certain, they were getting closer.

The original ticket collector approached the table and frowned. He bent over and collected the bag filled to the brim with pink tickets. The man removed his top hat and searched the ground for any wayward tickets. Every vote mattered. Once satisfied, he looked over at Vincent and asked, "What did I miss?"

***

"I knew the cookies would win. They were amazing," Madison grinned as she watched the blonde woman from earlier eagerly accept the Bake Off trophy. Her flushed cheeks and kind smile hinted at a well-earned win. The winner waved at the crowd and began a very lengthy acceptance speech.

Vincent laughed, "I knew Denise would win. She always has the best cookies. It's her signature move. I'm surprised she decided to try a new version of her famous recipe."

"You mean this isn't the typical winner?"

"Oh, she always wins. Her cookies are famous even in several towns over. What I'm saying is she did something different than usual. The cookies tasted more chocolaty than before."

Madison teased, "Chocolaty?"

"It might not be an official word, but it gets the point across."

"Fair enough. Now I need to visit her bakery."

Vincent laughed as the crowd around them clapped for the third-place runner-up. Children sat on their parent's shoulders and cheerfully joined the fun. Madison caught a glimpse of the possible future. A future that would require a little bit more balance between her personal and professional life. She'd figure it out. One step at a time.

For now, she needed to focus on solving an increasingly troublesome food mystery. The unknown man in a top hat proved they were headed in the right direction. He was getting desperate.

A streak of courage flooded her system. Eager to seize the momentum. Madison blurted out, "Can I stay over at your place tonight? Consider it a joint sleepover. Rocko would need to come over, too. I feed him breakfast pretty early."

For a moment, Vincent looked as if he was solving a math problem. Whatever equation he used, he came to the right answer.

"I have water and carrots. Tell Rocko to swing by the restaurant after dinner."

"Thank you."

Vincent shook his head, "Don't thank me. It's impossible to say no to Rocko."

His eyes held a teasing quality that settled Madison's previous nerves.

"I'll keep that in mind."

Vincent reached down and gripped Madison's hand. After a day filled with excitement, it felt nice to know that she wasn't alone. After months of living a relatively isolated existence, she'd unwittingly created an ecosystem of friends in a matter of weeks.

After months spent carrying everything on her own, Madison realized life felt a little less daunting surrounded by a group willing to help ease the load.

Chapter 25

The air outside of DeLuca's Restaurant weighed upon Madison's shoulders as her black cocktail dress did nothing to fight off the freezing temperatures. Even her favorite eggshell blue wool coat left her feeling exposed. The weather wasn't the only thing setting her senses on edge.

Madison hovered near the entrance as she tried to determine the gravity of the situation. She understood that something was about to change as soon as she opened the door. Whatever it was, she worried that she wasn't going to like it. But that wasn't going to stop her from finding out.

Her left hand tightened around the bottle of Pinot Noir as she pulled open DeLuca's front door. The brisk walk from her parked car to the restaurant felt like a cold plunge. Her teeth chattered as she looked around the restaurant.

A long white table spanned the length of the room. Small candles flickered in the center of the table, leaving enough room for the delicious food. The thoughtful gesture clogged the back of Madison's throat. How long had it taken for Vincent to put all of this together? At the very least, he spent most of yesterday preparing.

Vincent ambled over with his signature pink apron safely tied around his waist. He greeted, "Don't worry. The candles are battery-powered. I took that idea from your decor playbook. It makes the centerpieces completely childproof."

Vincent saw her blue skin and quickly wrestled off his apron. His previous train of thought was swiftly forgotten as soon as he saw

Madison's chilled face. He exclaimed, "You're freezing!"

"Not all the way. Only the top layer of skin."

"Very funny, let's put you near the wood-burning oven. Here."

Vincent walked over to a coat hanger and grabbed his jacket. He draped it over Madison's shoulders. His fingers lingered as the two of them stood together, cast in a warm crackling glow.

Madison thought back to the Ferris wheel. She looked into the flames and rubbed her hands together.

"Put your hands a little closer to the fire."

Unsure of the timing, she decided to keep the mood light. Her mouth curled into a smirk, "I have to warn you, I don't taste good."

Usually, Madison avoided making the odd cannibal joke, but around Vincent, it was as if all of her quirks didn't matter.

"Guess I'll just have to take your word for it. Let's get you warm."

Vincent guided Madison a little closer to the heat. His mind seemed distant as he thanked her for the bottle of wine and kept himself busy by rearranging the already perfectly plated appetizers. The mechanical gestures reminded Madison of her original question. Was this Vincent's way of throwing a goodbye party for his beloved restaurant?

Heat crept along the sides of Madison's neck as she undid her coat and held her hands near the state-of-the-art wood-burning oven.

"Speaking of cooking, I'm glad you're finally here. I need a taste tester."

A warm family-size portion of lasagna came out of the oven. Vincent carefully placed the steaming meal down and winked at Madison. While his spirits were dimmed, he was still trying to lighten the mood.

"This looks delicious."

Vincent laughed, "It is delicious. Recently inspired by someone I met."

"How could a person inspire a dish?"

"I guess you'll just have to try it at dinner and let me know." Vincent added, "It's a vegetarian lasagna. Each layer has a different vegetable and the sauce has a secret ingredient."

"Now I need to try it."

Vincent chuckled, "I can always count on you to solve a mystery."

Madison shrugged, "I like answers."

The conversation lulled as Vincent walked around the kitchen. His shoulders didn't seem as straight as usual.

She pressed, "What happened? I could feel your mood from outside of the restaurant."

"Maybe you're in the wrong profession. Have you ever thought about quitting the news and pursuing a career as a full-time detective?"

Madison laughed, "I'm taking your comment as a sign of agreement."

A tentative look passed across Vincent's features as his eyes quickly flicked to the apron discarded on the kitchen counter. He busied himself with the apron's strings for a few seconds longer than necessary.

Sensing his hesitation, she added, "You can talk to me whenever you want."

"How about later tonight once everyone's gone home?"

Madison's breath whispered out of her lungs. She watched as Vincent placed the finishing touches on a few appetizers. He kept his back intentionally turned to hide from Madison's perceptive gaze.

The heat thawed out her frozen digits within minutes. She walked over to the coat hangers and placed both of their coats away for the evening. Her black cocktail dress hugged her slight curves. Madison appreciated how the ruched stomach area of the dress showed off her waist. She rarely had the chance to wear such an elegant and well-cut dress. Although everything was covered, it wasn't what she personally felt would be appropriate for a television broadcast.

She had a sinking feeling that she knew what Vincent was about to say. Madison walked by DeLuca's several times during the week and each time the restaurant looked dead. Not a napkin out of place. At first, Madison had thought that Vincent had simply taken the week off to celebrate the Christmas Festival, but now she saw the bigger picture. The Christmas Festival was part of DeLuca's history. There was only one reason why Vincent would skip out on joining the local food stands.

The back of her throat felt dry as she forced out a simple, "I'd like that."

A bell chimed above the front door and newcomers brought new life into the room. Sneakers screeched against the spotless floor as Angie's voice asserted, "No running!"

A small head sped around the corner and joined Madison and Vincent in the kitchen. Max dug his heels into the floor as he skidded to a stop. Excitement danced in his eyes as he held up a handmade card. Crayon-colored people held hands on the cover of the paper card.

Max pointed to the green figure on the right and explained, "This is you, Madison."

His small finger moved to the other person as he continued, "And this is you, Vincent. I made this card to thank you for spending time with me."

Vincent walked over and grinned. He accepted the card and listened as Max intently explained the details hidden within the card. The conversations in the restaurant's seating area grew so loud that Max needed to raise his voice over the excited hum to be heard.

"It's perfect, Max."

"Will you put it in the restaurant so everyone will know how you helped me?"

Madison tried her best not to flinch once she saw the answer to her previous question so plainly reflected in Vincent's eyes. He swallowed, "For as long as the restaurant stands, Max."

"How about we help Vincent set the table?"

"Okay!"

Vincent sent Madison a knowing glance and nodded. It took every ounce of strength in Madison's body to stop herself from rushing forward and hugging Vincent.

"How can we help, Vincent?"

Vincent cleared his throat, "Max could you grab the bread baskets? Be careful, they're hot."

"Okay, easy."

Max sped out of the kitchen and left Madison and Vincent alone. The silence spoke volumes.

"What can I do Vincent?"

"You're already doing it."

"How?"

Vincent tucked a strand of hair behind Madison's ear as he confided, "You're standing next to me."

The heat from the oven incrementally increased in temperature. Madison's insides felt like they were burning up as she looked deep into Vincent's honest ocean eyes. The rarely seen dark stubble across his jaw emphasized his masculine features. She knew how much he preferred a clean look. Madison stepped forward and raised her hand to Vincent's jaw. She marveled at the roughened texture.

Vincent's eyes softened as he nuzzled his face into Madison's hand and asked, "Can you help me bring out the wine and appetizers?"

"Absolutely."

A small smile inched along Vincent's lips but it didn't reach his eyes. He walked over to a few intricately arranged serving platters and handed them to Madison. She carried a tray of mouthwatering fried arancini in one hand and a tray of delicious tomato bruschetta in the other.

Madison left the kitchen and admired her best friend. Angie donned a form-fitting gold dress that showed off her curvaceous full figure and effortlessly flowed with her movements. She looked wonderful.

Madison sent Angie a wink as she placed the appetizers on the table. Angie stood up and wrapped Madison in a warm hug.

Angie teased, "I love getting the chance to dress up. It's not every day that my husband comes home early from a work trip and my son scores the winning goal at a hockey game."

Hugh chuckled, "Talk about a work trip. I spent most of my time hiking all over Iceland."

"That explains the ruined snow boots."

"The stories I will tell you, Angie. First, let's celebrate with a delicious dinner."

"You can say that again, Hugh."

Vincent walked into the room with a generous selection of drinks effortlessly cradled within his arms. He joked, "I'm glad that all of my friends are food-motivated. It makes my job a little easier."

"I'm just happy I beat my hockey coach," Max waved at a few other locals as he returned to his mother's side. The intimate long table made it easy to see everyone without feeling overwhelmed.

"Do you remember our bet?"

Max enthusiastically nodded his head, "Cookies and bragging rights."

Vincent went around and poured everyone their preferred drink before he finally settled into his seat at the head of the table. He chuckled as he poured Max a generous helping of apple cider.

Max's dad noticed the slightly disappointed look etched along his son's face and joked, "Stick to the cookies, Max. They taste better."

Max pouted until Vincent returned from the kitchen with a tray overflowing with different types of cookies. The chocolate chips melted against Max's fingers as he pulled a warm chocolate chip cookie in half.

A sheepish look crossed Vincent's features as he looked over at Angie and Hugh. He winced, "Sorry, hope it's okay he has a little dessert before dinner."

Angie laughed as she waved her hand in the air. She looked over at her husband and grinned, "Sometimes exceptions need to be made. What better time than today."

Max's chin and lips were coated with chocolate. For such a small child, Madison had a sneaking suspicion that he could easily devour his body weight in chocolate. Given Vincent's massive cookie tray, it felt like the best time to test that theory. After dinner, of course.

Madison looked down the table and waved at a few now familiar faces. Matt and Nat looked over alongside the rest of Vincent's cousins and returned the friendly gesture.

A crooked smile inched across the corners of Madison's lips. She clapped her hands together as she raised a toast.

The table settled into a respectable silence as they waited for her to continue. Vincent sat to her right and stared at her with a caring look that would make the stars jealous of the brightness in his eyes.

"First, I'd like to thank Vincent for making this gathering possible. I don't think I've ever seen DeLuca's look so beautiful. Thank you for taking the time to prepare all of this delicious food. And Max, you did an amazing job today on the ice. A hockey rockstar in the making. When I look around this table, I don't just see friends, I see a wonderful extended family in the making. An extended family forged in adversity and bonded by food. To Max and Vincent."

"To Max and Vincent!"

Madison settled into her seat and watched Vincent's throat bob with emotion. He reached out and squeezed Madison's hand.

Vincent leaned over and whispered, "I'm going to remember this moment."

For some reason, Madison felt like his sentence held a weight that she couldn't fully grasp. She was certain of his candor but didn't recognize the intensity behind his words. He was deeply touched.

Madison leaned closer and added, "Let's do something to remember this moment."

For the second time, Madison stood up and waved her arms, "Let's take a group photo."

Angie raised her half-filled glass and cheered, "Approved!"

Hugh raced out the door before anyone could say another word. Madison exchanged a questioning look with Angie. Angie wiggled her eyebrows in a way that said: just wait.

The table descended into hushed pockets of conversation while Madison kept her gaze locked on the door. A chime rang through the room as Hugh returned with a spectacular camera and tripod in tow.

He sheepishly held up the photography equipment and explained, "I like to take wildlife photographs when on assignments."

Angie joked, "Honey, take a photo of this wildlife before we're properly stuffed."

One of Vincent's larger cousins laughed. He patted his partner's shoulder as the two broke into lighthearted conversation.

Hugh easily arranged his camera and explained, "I put it on a timer. We will have 10 seconds before the flash. Say pasta."

"Pasta!"

Dinner included an abundance of delicious carbs and sweets. Every time Madison thought she couldn't take another bite, Vincent brought out another dish. Eventually, he brought out the vegetarian lasagna and sent Madison a teasing wink. She took a generous serving and anticipated a typical Italian dish. To her surprise, the lasagna tasted slightly sweet. She tentatively took another bite as she tried to place the taste.

Her eyes lit up with recognition. Vincent really did listen.

Madison whispered to Vincent as he circulated around the guests, "Apples."

"Can't put anything past you."

The two stood next to each other as they listened to Vincent's cousins retell stories of distant Christmas Eves. It was a jovial event filled with mouthwatering food and good company.

Once the final friend exited the restaurant, Madison sighed and settled into one of the booths near the front while Vincent reorganized the tables. She had offered to help but had quickly been shooed away. Madison wasn't about to argue against avoiding manual labor. Instead, she settled into the leather seat and gave her feet a rest. On a deeper level, she didn't want to rush the moment.

Once the final chair was put away and the last glass was carefully placed into the dishwasher, Madison knew it was time. She walked over to Vincent and waved her car keys in the air. A curious look crossed her face as she asked, "Can you drive?"

"Sure, I didn't drink."

"Why not?"

He cleared his throat, "I knew I'd be driving you to pick up Rocko before coming back to spend the night at my place."

"How did you know I wouldn't have Rocko with me?"

She already knew the answer as soon as the question left her lips. It was a good thing she wasn't driving.

Vincent chuckled as he placed his jacket over Madison's shoulders. He locked the restaurant as they exited into the frigid night air.

He teased, "A lucky guess."

"Maybe you should be the future detective."

"Just for tonight."

Chapter 26

"Lenny, what do you think about this angle?"

Several rows of shiny new hardcover books glinted in the background of the upcoming news segment. The scent of new paint lingered in the air as the freshly remodeled shop proudly prepared to welcome a remarkable influx of eager readers.

"I think it looks smart, but the lighting could be better. Give me a few minutes to fix it."

Madison nodded her head and mentally agreed with Lenny. The dull orange glow coming through the front window could be better. When it came to cameras, Lenny was the best. He knew how to work with pretty much anything that had a lens. The channel even asked him to help with investigative segments because he loved to innovate discreet cameras. People at work still talked about how Lenny turned a small hand puppet into a portable camera. Madison turned her attention elsewhere while her coworker worked his magic.

The snow outside looked about ankle-deep and was projected to stay on the ground for at least a few more days. A meek white-haired woman in her early forties stood against the shop's cool window. The back of her frilly shirt brushed against the spotless glass. Wide-rimmed glasses framed her birdlike features and created an owlish appearance. If Madison squinted, the white frills of the woman's shirt closely resembled pale ruffled feathers.

"Mrs. Fullbright, thank you for allowing us to film in your store. Before we start, would you like to tell me more about why you decided to open the bookstore in Lakewood? I read online that you lived two towns over."

Thin lips pressed together as Mrs. Fullbright prepared to reply. After a brief pause, she squawked, "I wanted to make a bookstore for people who love to cook. Lakewood has a reputation for being one of the best places to eat so it felt like a logical place to open my shop."

"What do you mean?"

"About half of the fictional books in this store are cooking-related. The shelves on the back walls are all cookbooks. If you want a fictional book about cooking or something cooking-related then search closer to the middle of the store."

Mrs. Fullbright waved her hands from one side of the room to the other. The frills on her shirt shifted with the movement and gave the impression that she was moments away from taking flight.

Madison nodded and tried to understand the shop's unconventional name. She pressed, "Is that why you named the store Sweet Pages?"

"Yes, I thought it sounded unique. My niece helped me come up with the idea."

"Oh?"

"You might have heard of her, Denise Raymonds. She's pretty famous in Lakewood for her bakery and cookie recipe. Do you know her?"

"Not personally, but now you've given me a great reason to keep an eye out for her. Anyone with an excellent cookie or pie recipe is a friend of mine."

Curiosity heightened Madison's attention. She regretted not taking the time to get to know more people. When it came to socializing, it wasn't like her cabin carefully tucked into the woods was doing her any favors. Speaking of her home, Madison needed to head back and feed Rocko as soon as she finished this interview. The local locksmith had been more than accommodating and agreed to change all of the locks for a bargain. She absently patted the shiny new key while she watched Lenny put the finishing touches on the lighting. A bright glow illuminated the multi-colored book spines and Madison caught a few of the names. One book entitled *Cozy Chocolate Christmas Cakes* touched another labeled *Happy Seasonal Delicious Delights*. Madison assumed the books were popular given the significant volume stacked tightly into a middle shelf.

"Are those two books popular?"

Madison nudged her microphone in the direction of the two recipe books. Mrs. Fullbright smiled as she pushed the bridge of her glasses further up her nose.

"Both books were published by Denise. I guess you could say that I'm a proud relative. She has the best Festival Famous Christmas Cookies in town."

Mrs. Fullbright leaned closer to Madison as she added, "Her award-winning recipes aren't included in the books, of course."

A lightbulb turned on in the back of Madison's mind. Something about Mrs. Fullbright's sentence had Madison's brain crackling with energy.

"Ready when you are, Madison."

Lenny's voice pushed her into the present moment. She sent Mrs. Fullbright a reassuring grin and prepared to highlight Sweet Pages' culinary slant.

"I hope this goes well. My days are usually spent with my nose tucked into a book."

Madison empathized with Mrs. Fullbright's interview nerves. She knew some people tended to feel shy around all of the bright lights and cameras. Luckily, it was a relatively private setting and Madison felt confident that she could guide Mrs. Fullbright through it.

"You'll be great."

Mrs. Fullbright's large eyes turned to Madison as she warbled, "How do you know?"

"Because I'll make sure of it."

***

As expected, the interview concluded without a hitch. Towards the end, Mrs. Fullbright practically glowed with pride as she showed off her new bookshelves and extensive cooking-friendly selection.

"Thank you for the interview, Madison."

A warm glow spread through Madison's chest as she stood a bit taller than before. She shook Mrs. Fullbright's hand and joked, "You did all of the hard work. It was a great idea to mention the history of the building. I didn't know that it used to be an old chocolate factory."

"Yes! It was one of the first commercial structures built within the center of Lakewood. I knew it was mine from the moment I laid eyes on the tiled floors and carved wooden walls"

Lenny was already at the news van. He took pride in organizing his equipment between news segments. The news cycle felt never-ending which was surprising for a town as cozy and quaint as Lakewood. Luckily, Madison had a few days off.

Madison reached for the door handle and prepared to wave goodbye. Like a bolt of lightning, she made an electrifying connection.

"Festival Famous Ooey Gooey Christmas Cookies."

"I'm sorry?"

The bottom of Madison's pink coat spun around her ankles as she whirled to face Mrs. Fullbright. An excited gleam danced in her eyes while she explained, "By any chance was one of Denise's famous recipes called Festival Famous Ooey Gooey Christmas Cookies?"

Mrs. Fullbright's eyes squinted as she stumbled over her words. Her mouth opened and closed as her tongue ran over her next sentence before it even had legs to crawl.

"I don't know. It sounds familiar. I do know her famous recipe mentions something like Gooey. What's wrong? Is she in trouble?"

"No! Nothing like that. Would you be able to identify her handwriting? I took a photo of a handwritten recipe card."

"That could be Denise. She likes to write down her recipes as she goes. I think it's part of her baking genius."

Madison nodded as she pulled out her phone and scrolled through her recent photos. It wasn't lost on her that in the last few weeks, she'd taken more photos than her entire camera roll combined. Maybe, she'd finally slowed down enough to appreciate the view instead of just filming it.

Looped cursive neatly sprawled along an index card flashed across her screen. Madison flicked back to the recipe. She looked at Mrs.

Fullbright and wondered if it would be right to share someone's private recipe with a stranger. Given the odd circumstances surrounding how the recipe fell into Madison's possession, she was willing to guess it counted as an exception. Still, she zoomed in just enough to conceal the last two bottom lines of the recipe.

"Would you mind looking at this for a moment?"

Mrs. Fullbright adjusted her glasses and looked at Madison's phone screen. Tension built within the room as Madison waited for the confirmation that she so desperately wanted to hear. One tense second slipped into another as she waited for Mrs. Fullbright's approval.

"Your phone screen is locked."

"Oh," Madison flipped her phone around and punched in her passcode. She turned the screen back to Mrs. Fullbright.

A startled noise escaped the back of Mrs. Fullbright's throat as her eyes darted from one portion of the recipe to another.

"That's Denise's handwriting. I don't understand how you managed to take a photo of her most popular cookie recipe. She hasn't even shown it to me. I would never tell anyone though since I'm a strong supporter of culinary creators."

Satisfaction flooded Madison's veins as she returned her phone back into her jacket pocket. A satisfied smile played at the edges of her lips as she replied, "That's exactly what I plan to find out. The recipe was found somewhere it didn't belong. I'll be sure to return it to Denise. I guess this solves one mystery."

"What mystery?"

"Well, everyone at the Christmas Festival said that her cookie recipe tasted different than usual. A few locals thought that she was just trying out a new twist. Now it all makes sense. She didn't have the recipe card so she had to remake the cookies from memory. Don't worry, she still won first place."

Mrs. Fullbright grinned, "I know my niece. She has a way of creating the best sweets from even the most sour situations."

Madison watched as Mrs. Fullbright opened and closed her mouth. Her thin lips pressed together as if she wanted to swallow her next sentence.

"What is it?"

Two large eyes carefully searched around the room before returning to Madison's face. Mrs. Fullbright tutted, "It's a silly thought, but I like to think that in some ways most creative fields have a lot in common. A recipe tells a story while also explaining a process. It's similar to writing a work of fiction. The best part is that the story being told never changes, but the readers do with time."

"I agree. Whenever I reread a book, I find new meanings or nuances I missed the first time."

"Exactly. I like to think that's part of the magic. Sometimes we're able to see new things we might have missed the first time."

"I think you've just inspired me to start reading more often."

Mrs. Fullbright laughed as the tension within her shoulders loosened. She nodded, "Come into the store, anytime."

"Thank you, Mrs. Fullbright. I better get back to Lenny."

Madison left the shop and thought over the recent development. Denise owned one of the most popular bakeries in town. Had she broken into Madison's home and intentionally left her famous recipe behind to keep Madison off her trail? Denise probably knew she could win the Bake Off even without using her original recipe. It was an unlikely move, but not impossible. Had Denise hired someone to steal the Bake Off votes to make sure that she'd win? If so, who was she working with? Sweetie's Bakery had a constant flow of customers. Maybe the new bakery was too much competition. Madison decided that she needed to meet Denise before placing her at the top of her list of suspects.

The puzzle was slowly coming together. Little did Madison know that she was missing the final piece.

Chapter 27

Rocko zipped around his enclosure as Madison hovered over her computer screen. She'd finished her news shift and rushed back to Vincent's. Even with the locks fixed, she felt safer staying at Vincent's place.

After the dinner party, Vincent gave Madison his bedroom. He'd insisted on sleeping in his home office if his desk covered with stacks of paper and his well-stocked bookshelves were anything to go by.

The odd encounter with the unknown Christmas Festival ticket thief made them both a little uneasy. While Vincent hadn't brought it up, the event remained fresh in both of their minds.

Madison still couldn't remember where she had seen the imposter ticket collector before. Her inability to recall his face was mentally driving her up Vincent's shell-colored walls. She sucked in a deep breath and looked away from the computer screen. Madison took comfort in the knowledge that she wasn't alone. Well, technically she was since Vincent was out getting groceries, but it felt better to cohabitate under the current circumstances.

In true Vincent fashion, he hadn't insisted one way or the other. He had simply placed a fresh change of sheets outside of the bedroom door and bought an impressive selection of feminine toiletries. The jumbo-sized vanilla-scented shampoo and conditioner would safely last Madison through the week.

Madison groaned as she rubbed her eyes and frowned at her computer screen. She refocused her attention on her little fluffy friend.

"What do you think, Rocko?"

She'd replayed the footage from DeLuca's Restaurant over and over. Still, Madison couldn't figure out how Rocko had entered the shop. According to the footage, it looked like Rocko had managed to pry open the door just enough to squeeze through. Given the weight of DeLuca's front door, Madison had a hard time accepting the theory. She was missing something.

"Maybe we need to watch it one more time. What did Mrs. Fullbright say about different perspectives? Let's see if we have a better angle."

Madison begrudgingly grabbed the computer and arranged it on the floor. She placed her phone next to the computer and paused. Madison watched her image as it reflected off her darkened phone screen. Inspired, she hastily replayed the footage. Instead of looking at the front door, she focused on the interior of DeLuca's. She focused on a small mirror proudly perched between a few of Vincent's family photos. After a few seconds, a dark blotch flickered in the mirror moments before Rocko seemingly managed to open the front door.

"Someone crawled below the windows and put Rocko inside of the restaurant."

Madison tapped the carpet as she replayed the video and slowed down the speed. She zoomed in and paused.

She couldn't believe the side profile caught looking at her. Oddly, it all made sense. Half of Madison wanted to sprint down the street and confront the person illuminated on the screen. The more logical part of her copied the footage and prepared to come up with a plan.

Of course, the main part of having a plan usually included having to throw it out the window.

Chapter 28

"Thank you for agreeing to help, Mrs. Fullbright."

Mrs. Fullbright's outfit looked even more outrageous than before. Madison had a sneaking suspicion that her companion had toned down her usual attire during her interview. Today, Mrs. Fullbright wore a bedazzled golden knee-length skirt and a bell-sleeved purple shirt. Her sleeves were so long that she looked about five seconds from taking a technicolored flight. In comparison, Denise wore blue denim jeans and a black turtleneck.

Mrs. Fullbright nodded while her niece eagerly jumped into the conversation, "Thank you for including us! My aunt told me about your plan. I hope you don't mind that I wanted to tag along."

Madison laughed, "The more, the merrier. Just remember to stay quiet once he comes into the store. We don't want him to know that anything is off."

"Sure thing. I just wanted to see the person who tried to kidnap my famous cookie recipe. Thanks again for returning it to me, Madison."

"You're brave," Mrs. Fullbright stated as she flew behind the curtain that separated the back of the store from the front. While willing to help, it was obvious Mrs. Fullbright was less than eager to take part in the upcoming confrontation.

Secretly, Madison was terrified. She'd spent most of the night considering alternatives but none of them sounded fast enough. A verbal confession from the culprit would help to speed up an investigation. Vincent didn't have the luxury of time. Neither did the other eateries on the edge of financial ruin. It was now or never.

For everything to work, Madison needed to bluff. She didn't have all of the evidence but that's where the confession would come in. At least, that's what Madison hoped would happen. Mrs. Fullbright and Denise would be right behind the curtain, listening to the entire conversation.

Madison offered Denise a small smile as the other woman proceeded behind the curtain. The books stood guard as Madison waited for the perfect opportunity to put her plan into action. The bookstore's front window faced the new bakery across the street. Even with the majority of the other eateries in town closed, the place had less than a handful of customers pushing dry day-old cake from one side of their plate to the other. Even from across the street, it was a sorry sight to see.

As soon as the clock struck five, the owner shooed everyone out. He even waved his hands in the air and squabbled with a mother as she tried to console her crying child. The unfriendly actions didn't exactly scream business owner of the year. Still, the man's eagerness to leave for the day didn't exactly shout criminal of the year, either. That's where Madison's plan hopefully got the ball rolling.

At five minutes after five, a slender form locked the purple bakery's front door and slunk down the street. It was Madison's chance. She watched as he crossed the street and headed over to his car parked just outside of the bookstore.

Madison schooled her features and prepared to get closer. She stepped outside of the store and met Mr. Art's beady eyes. Recognition flashed behind his dark gaze before he shoved it away.

She spoke in a cool tone, "I know what you're doing to the other restaurants. If you don't want me to turn you in, you'll speak with me somewhere private."

For a moment, Madison wasn't sure he'd take the bait. He stood next to his vehicle while his car keys jingled against the door handle.

"Not here."

Art inspected the street and pushed open the bookstore's front door. A sign on the door claimed that Mrs. Fullbright was on a break. Given the friendly nature of everyone in town, it wasn't uncommon for shopkeepers to leave their stores unlocked while they meandered down the road for a bite to eat. After everything that had happened in the last few weeks, the trusting gesture now felt comical.

Art cautiously walked down an aisle and inspected the back of the store for eavesdroppers. Madison's heart jumped into overdrive as he inched closer to the curtain.

"Well, are you going to speak with me or are you going to keep looking at books?"

Bingo.

Art hovered near the Halloween-related culinary books. His fingers lingered on a book where the cannolis looked like the spindly fingers of a witch. How fitting. His presence definitely spooked Madison.

He walked back to the front of the store and appraised Madison. His nose stuck into the air as he questioned, "Did you recently learn how to make chocolate cookies?"

The question seemed so innocent that Madison wouldn't have understood the innuendo if she hadn't personally dealt with the situation. He had broken into her little cabin and dropped the stolen cookie recipe. A spark of awareness jolted down Madison's spine as she stood her ground.

As far as admissions of guilt went, that was pretty weak. He hadn't said anything out of the ordinary, especially so soon after the Christmas Festival.

Madison arched a brow, "Maybe. Given your empty bakery, it looks like you haven't made any winning recipes."

Her comment wiped the pleased smirk clean off Art's face. Worth it. She decided to press her luck. Maybe if she pushed enough, he'd admit to stealing the recipe. Or confess to breaking into Sweetie's Bakery. Or better yet, admit to calling the health department after putting Rocko inside DeLuca's.

"Have you considered moving to a town with less competition? It could increase your chances of having a few desperate customers."

Fury etched along the small man's face. Madison imagined steam rolling out of both of his ears. He took a step closer and hissed, "You don't have any proof."

Madison raised her chin and kept her features cool. Her eyes remained locked on the man only a few feet away. Although he looked harmless, Madison knew the truth. Anyone willing to tamper with a ladder was capable of horrible things. Madison paused midstream of consciousness.

Wait.

Whoever was behind the restaurant closures wouldn't expect Madison to use the ladder. No. A rush of adrenaline shot through her body as soon as she connected the dots. The broken ladder was intended for another restaurant owner. Madison had unwittingly prevented a tragic accident from happening to Vincent. Validation warmed her heart once she realized Vincent wasn't behind the food-focused mayhem. Her gut was right. There was no way Vincent was working with Art.

She kept her composure by remembering Denise and Mrs. Fullbright were only a few feet away. Surely, he was outnumbered.

"You'll be sorry." Art stared Madison down as spittle flew into the air. He sped across the store and yanked open the front door. Madison watched as he hopped into his car and sped away.

Denise poked her head outside of the curtain. She asked, "Is he gone?"

"For now."

Denise groaned, "He's definitely guilty."

Mrs. Fullbright pulled back the curtain just far enough so that she could poke her head out. She nervously inspected the shelves before she whispered, "He's horrible."

Denise laughed, "A menace to the culinary community."

Madison leaned against one of the shelves as her shoulders deflated. Disappointment colored her tone as she added, "I'm sorry. For a reporter, I really failed to catch a confession."

Mrs. Fullbright shook her head. The movement rattled the curtain that her fingers clutched in an iron grip. She whispered, "This went better than I expected."

Madison laughed, "What were you expecting?"

A shaky voice quivered, "Homicide."

Denise arched a brow, "Over a cookie recipe?"

Mrs. Fullbright looked at her niece and amended, "I try to avoid getting between a person and their passion."

"Murder isn't a passion project. He's a career criminal masquerading as a baker." Denise turned to Madison as she arched a brow, expecting some backup.

Unwilling to get between family, Madison figured it was best to redirect the energy bubbling within the bookstore. She didn't want to end the attempted sleuthing party on a bad note. Madison suggested, "Why don't we head over to DeLuca's and talk it over?"

A bundle of white frizzy hair incrementally inched further away from the curtain as Mrs. Fullbright agreed, "I could eat."

Denise nodded as she tapped her fingers against the checkout counter, deep in thought. She hummed in the back of her throat and looked around the room.

Madison asked, "What are you thinking?"

"I'm thinking this went about as well as the first time that I tried to make my famous Peanut Butter Brittle Cookies."

Mrs. Fullbright snorted as she cautiously crept out of the back room. She looked between Madison and Denise with a comical spark of laughter in her eyes.

Madison pressed, "Am I missing something?"

Denise admitted, "Yeah, my kitchen caught on fire."

Chapter 29

"Hi, Vincent."

A head of thick hair popped up from sorting through one of the kitchen cabinets. He looked over at the excited trio and grinned.

"Did Madison convince you to eat here?"

Denise rolled her eyes.

"Oh yeah, practically shoved us through your heavy front door. It has nothing to do with the fact that DeLuca's is the best sit-down restaurant in Lakewood."

Vincent chuckled as he walked into the dining area with a pitcher of water in tow. He made a wide gesture to the mostly empty tables.

Denise selected a booth closer to the middle of the restaurant. While the ladies were busy debating the menu, Madison looked up and shot Vincent a cheesy grin.

He always had a natural air of confidence around him but it was another thing to watch him in his element. Vincent shined as he moved from one table to the next and kept the food coming. For only one person, he kept the restaurant moving like a well-oiled machine.

The breadbasket arrived right as Madison's stomach let out the whale call of the century. Mrs. Fullbright looked embarrassed on Madison's behalf while Denise acted like nothing had happened.

"You ladies definitely worked up an appetite. I'd say lunch can't come a minute too soon."

Denise rolled up the sleeves of her dark turtleneck before she tucked into the breadbasket. She snapped a long spindly breadstick in half.

"You can say that again. We worked for our meal today. Especially Madison. Madison earned her share of the breadbasket."

"Oh really?"

For some reason, Madison knew this wasn't going to end well. She looked down at her cup of water and took a lingering sip.

Denise proceeded to fill Vincent in on their failed operation. Potential human sacrifice (Madison) to Art and all.

Madison wondered if all of the ice water in the restaurant would be able to cool down her burning cheeks.

Chapter 30

Vincent didn't say a word. He opened and closed his mouth like a fish. If he had fins, Madison was pretty sure he'd be sinking to the bottom of the tank.

"What's wrong, Vincent? You didn't think it was him?"

Denise's friendly comment snapped Vincent out of his floundering. He opted for a verbal life raft and joked, "I wasn't expecting that."

Madison saw right through the friendly quip. She knew better than to press that matter in public. The topic would eventually come back up once they were at Vincent's house.

For the last few days, they'd settled into a relaxing routine. Vincent baked cookies before bed and Madison prepared a small pot of coffee. While unconventional, the small tasks offered a bit of structure to their nightly routine. Madison liked the idea of coming home to someone eager to hear about her day. Her nightly routine now included some of the best cookies in town.

Denise recounted the entire bookstore bombardment with surprising accuracy given that she was hidden behind a curtain for the duration of the confrontation. The entire time, Madison hoped the fire alarm in the kitchen would short-circuit or the ice maker would suddenly become possessed. Anything to stop the words from coming out of Denise's detail-oriented mouth.

The impromptu chat grew more animated as Vincent pulled up a chair next to the booth. He placed his chin into the palm of his hand and added, "What else happened?"

Denise kept going.

Maybe Madison could start a small fire in the bathroom using the two-ply. She was getting desperate. It wasn't that she didn't want Vincent to know. No, it was more that she didn't want him to worry. To be fair, she was currently staying at his house because she was so worried about her safety. Maybe it was a combination of factors. Madison knew she probably should have filled Vincent in before jumping into her plan. For some reason, it felt dishonest for Denise to be telling Vincent the story. Madison felt like he should have heard it from her.

Vincent turned his head and noticed a table in the corner needing a few refills. Before he left, his eyes connected with Madison's. His meaning was clear. Madison subtly nodded her head. They'd talk about this later.

The meal came and went in a blur of conversation. At one point, Madison excused herself to the bathroom. The idea of creating a crazed toilet paper fire was sounding better by the minute. She finished up and stared into the mirror. Her sweaty palms gripped the sides of the ceramic sink as she gathered her nerves. She'd messed up.

Madison returned to the table as Mrs. Fullbright and her niece exchanged an odd look. Madison dismissed it as a family spat. She slipped back into the middle of the chat while Denise took the lead. Her new friend's excitement was understandable. Denise's famous cookie recipe was safely back in her possession and the person responsible for the theft seemed only a hair-lengths away from justice.

Mrs. Fullbright's purple shirt went up Madison's nose as the two hugged goodbye.

Slowly, Madison turned around. She felt like a naughty child caught with her hand in the cookie jar. Madison considered leaving the restaurant but figured it was better to nip the impending conversation in the bud. Vincent calmly appeared around the kitchen counter and locked eyes with Madison. Mentally, Madison envisioned the theme song for the Titanic as she marched to the back of the restaurant. It was time to face the music.

Chapter 31

"Is Denise serious?"

Vincent folded his arms across his chest and leaned against the counter. His posture practically pulled an explanation from the tip of Madison's tongue. Almost. She bit down and sighed.

"Yes, but it was completely safe. Mrs. Fullbright and Denise hid in the back room. I spoke with Art while they acted as backup. The worst part is I know he's guilty but I can't prove it."

Vincent inhaled and shifted his weight. He looked stuck between a rock and a hard place. He said, "Maybe it would be better to let it go."

Madison stepped back. She felt like she'd been emotionally punched in the chest. Let it go? She had prepared a speech promising to include him the next time she decided to investigate. Madison hadn't prepared for Vincent to tell her to let it go. She didn't know how to interpret his words. Did he think she wasn't capable of discovering the culprit?

Pain radiated around her heart as she pondered Vincent's suggestion. Let it go? What was he talking about? Did Vincent think she couldn't handle herself?

Sure, she was a younger reporter and spent most of her time speaking to animal rescues and store owners, but she could also handle more complex stories. She was willing to put in the time necessary to become great. Madison didn't move to Lakewood to avoid a challenge. No, she moved here to embrace the next chapter in her life and everything that came with it.

She bristled, "Don't worry about me, Vincent. I always figure it out. I thought you would understand that this investigation is important to me."

Madison couldn't hide the pain dancing behind her eyes. She took a step back and mumbled, "I'll get Rocko from your house and leave the spare key under your doormat."

She turned on her heel and retreated out of the restaurant. Tears threatened to fall as she struggled to keep it together. As soon as the cool air kissed her cheeks, the floodgates broke loose. With Christmas less than a few days away, Madison wondered if she had made the right choice. She knew it would be easy to walk away from the final parts of her self-imposed investigation, but she was just too close.

Madison felt like she owed it to the people in town to finish. She also owed it to herself. Living in Lakewood meant being part of a community greater than herself. This mystery impacted innocent people and Madison knew she could put an end to it. Still, a seed of doubt threatened to grow in the back of her mind.

Maybe Vincent was right. She hadn't proceeded with much caution. Her silent drive over to Vincent's house gave her a moment to think. His two-story brick home sat on a quiet cul-de-sac. Madison loved the sense of community. Hand-painted mailboxes lined the street. She drove past a few names carefully looped in cursive while others were messily printed and slanted to the left.

Madison slowed down as the makings of another plan popped into her head. She parked in Vincent's driveway and sped inside.

She walked into Vincent's room and searched her belongings for the handwritten threatening letter. She pulled it out of one of her detective books and read it in the waning light. This was it. She just needed to compare the note with Art's handwriting. How was she going to get an original copy of his writing? It wasn't like she was on the best terms with her number one suspect.

She called up Angie as she collected her belongings. Her heart raced with excitement as she greeted, "Hi Angie, I have a small favor."

Chapter 32

"I can't tell if this is the dumbest thing I've ever done or the best thing I've ever done."

Angie agreed, "I like to think that there's a fine line between genius and stupidity."

"Wait, isn't there a saying about that? Doesn't matter. Thanks for helping me, Angie."

"Like I said, ask and I'll be there."

Angie's fake mustache lost its adhesive and slipped down her lips. The fake hair looked like something from a bad 80s cops show. The wardrobe department for a local news channel was a far cry from a Hollywood film set budget. The mustache just needed to be reglued. Madison knew that they could make it work. The shoulder pads on Angie's suit? Not so much.

After a full hour perusing the wardrobe department, the duo felt confident that it was the best that they were going to get. Which wasn't saying much.

"I look like a sickly English professor," Madison took in her disguise and huffed.

"Well, get into character. If you're a sickly English professor then I look like a failed art student living in my mother's basement."

"Not exactly the most promising backstories for our disguises."

Madison stood next to Angie in the full-length mirror and laughed. She snapped a photo and sent it in the group chat with Lenny and Angie. Hopefully, they'd be able to look back on this moment and laugh. They looked ridiculous. Who would believe these costumes?

Angie pushed, "Look, we don't need to have the most believable backstories. We're ordering pastries from a store and recording Art when he writes down our orders."

"How do you know he writes his orders by hand?"

A knowing smile lifted the left corner of Angie's beleaguered mustache. She applied a fresh layer of glue and spoke around the fake hair.

"Everyone who goes into the store complains about it. He writes most of his orders down wrong and it's something that annoys anyone considering becoming a regular. It's easier to order a delicious strudel from Sweetie's Bakery than deal with his messy handwriting."

Madison held back a laugh as she pressed, "So you're everyone?"

Angie looked at Madison through the mirror and admitted, "In this specific situation, yes."

Madison agreed, "Sweetie's Bakery has the best strudel in town."

"I told you that when you first moved here."

"Okay, let's check the equipment one last time."

The two walked outside of the small dressing room and met Lenny in the hallway. He sat in a plastic chair casually eating a footlong turkey sandwich. Angie and Madison smacked the door open and Lenny jerked his knee. Crumbs littered the floor as he stood to his feet.

Madison grabbed a lint roller and picked up the excess crumbs in one easy roll. She looked back at Lenny and said, "Thanks for agreeing to do this."

"Don't mention it. My little kiddo is in school for a few more hours so it's no problem. Her winter break is really late this year."

Angie commiserated, "I know the feeling. It's great for last-minute Christmas shopping but not so great when it comes to spending time together. Want to know what's the worst?"

"Lay it on me," Lenny said between the final bites of his meal.

"I'm scheduled to work Christmas morning. Hugh just got home and we were looking forward to spending the day together as a family."

Madison didn't even hesitate as she offered, "I'll take your shift, Angie."

"That's amazing, Madison. Are you sure? You've already done so much for us."

Madison teased, "I could use the extra shift. Don't we get a little bonus for every holiday that we cover?"

"Yes, but I don't know if that's worth working through Christmas."

Madison refused to budge, "Angie, I want to help. You're giving up your free time to help me put together a self-directed news pitch. We don't even know if people will want to watch investigative reporting in a small town."

"Have a little faith."

"I'm working on it."

Lenny stood from his seat and held out what looked like a normal pair of glasses and a ballpoint pen. He gave Madison the glasses and Angie the pen. Lenny looked between the two and explained, "Madison's palms get sweaty."

Madison laughed, "Good point."

Lenny added, "It also helps to hide your distinctive features."

"It's a deviated septum."

"That's not what I was talking about. I was thinking that Art already knows your face. We don't have the budget for colored eye contacts or fancy prosthetics so mustaches and glasses will need to work."

Angie placed a hand on her hip and brushed her fingers over her fake mustache. She joked, "This is like a budget spy movie."

Madison frowned, "How do we use the glasses and pen?"

"Right. Point the glasses and pen in the direction you want to record. Click the pen to start recording. The glasses just need to be pushed up the bridge of your nose. They're pretty easy to use."

"I still can't believe our boss gave us the green light for this."

Angie teased, "It helped that you made a slideshow and sent out a video along with a playlist with over 50 different cooking-related songs."

Lenny chuckled, "I liked the title of the playlist. Christmas Culinary Caper."

Madison groaned as they headed out to their rental car. They didn't want to park their real cars near the bakery, in case Art recognized them. It felt a bit over the top, but Madison was committed to pulling out all the stops their tiny budget allowed.

She unlocked the blue SUV and asked, "Ready?"

Chapter 33

Her palms were sweaty just like Lenny had predicted. She wiped her hands down the sides of her shapeless pants but the moisture returned as quickly as it disappeared. Madison stared at the purple highlighter-colored walls of Art's Bakery. Unsurprisingly, only one customer sat near the back of the eatery. Her computer glowed as she made the most of the place's internet.

Madison didn't get it. How could a place with so little competition still be so empty? In a matter of minutes, she was about to find out. Ready or not.

Lenny sat in the backseat of the ocean-colored vehicle while he noshed on a bright red licorice twist. He looked at Madison's pale face and frowned.

"Want one?"

"No, thanks. We're about to buy a bunch of random treats from a bakery. Do you want anything?"

Angie teased, "Yeah, we're taking requests."

Lenny hummed in the back of his throat as he considered his options. In true Lenny fashion, he took his time.

To be fair, Madison wasn't in any rush. She preferred the comfort of the rental car. It was safe and predictable. Investigating a bakery run by a man who almost indirectly killed her with a ladder? Not so much. Madison morbidly thought if he did try something, at least it would be caught on camera.

Angie didn't feel the same way. She looked at her phone and pressed, "We only have a few more hours before we need to get the kids from school."

"How about a blueberry muffin and a lemon scone?"

"Done deal, Lenny. Keep the getaway car warm."

The sentence rang around the car as Angie effortlessly hopped out of the rental's passenger door. Madison didn't know why she felt so nervous. She'd already confronted Art once. Maybe this time felt different because they were entering his territory. Then again, Lenny planned to supervise from the car and Angie was already walking over to the bakery's door at a breakneck speed.

An unexpected wave of confidence washed through Madison's body as she pushed the glasses up the bridge of her nose and sped after Angie. It was time to get to work.

Poorly lit food display cases commanded the center of the bakery. Madison tried her best not to wrinkle her nose. Maybe the food was perfectly fine. Not every baker knew how to showcase their confections. Madison inched closer to the front of the store and looked inside the cases.

Never mind.

Art sat on a bench while he hunched over a magazine. He didn't look up when Angie and Madison approached.

A Western accent broke the silence. Angie drawled, "Afternoon. We were just passing through and noticed your delightful-looking confectionary. We'd like to rustle up a few snacks for the road."

What.

Madison was so shocked by the accent that she almost forgot to angle her head in Art's direction. She hoped her head movements were slow enough for the camera in the plastic glasses to keep up.

While Angie kept the conversation going, Madison angled her body to keep Art in her sights. She leaned forward and listened as Angie listed off a few bakery items for Lenny.

Between instructions, Angie clicked the top of the tiny pen and placed it poking out of her jacket's pocket. The tiny camera pointed in the direction of the yellow-tinted treats.

An annoyed voice snapped, "We don't have any blueberry muffins or lemon scones. Look in the case and pick something."

"How about one of these?"

Oh, no. Madison couldn't stop it. She'd somehow turned into a fake Canadian who summered in New Jersey. The accent was horrible. Any second now, he'd recognize her and insist the poorly disguised duo leave the shop.

To her surprise, Art sighed and slid off the stool behind the counter. His shop looked so soullessly arranged. All four interior walls matched the fluorescent shade of purple covering the exterior walls. It reminded Madison of someone who liked to flip through magazines for ideas but couldn't fully connect the dots. The shop lacked the warmth the other eateries around town effortlessly possessed. Of course, Madison had every reason to be biased.

He pushed open one of the bakery cases and grabbed a day-old brownie using a wooden spoon. Madison wasn't being fair. She didn't know for sure that it was a day-old brownie. The brownie just didn't look fresh or appealing.

Oh no.

Madison realized he wasn't writing anything down. Without handwritten evidence, they wouldn't be able to prove Art was guilty.

"We're looking to make a big order so we can enjoy lots of sweets while on the road. How about one of these, two of those, and four of these? Oh, what about the rice treats on the top shelf? Are they fresh? Who cares? Not me. Let's do three. Don't forget the slices of chocolate cake in the other case. We'll take two. Do you have coffee? Let's add two coffees and one of those coffee-looking cakes."

Madison fleetingly checked the case for apple pie and stopped short. She told herself she'd just have to buy a slice of pie another time. An undercover investigation was not the time to get distracted.

Art waved his hands in the air and sprinted to the register. He returned with a notebook and yelped, "Slow down! Let me write this down."

Mason grinned and covered it with the sleeve of her oversized suit. She watched as Art's pen refused to work. He furiously scribbled on the side of the paper until a bit of ink finally decided to cooperate.

He looked up at Madison and asked, "One more time, please."

A surprisingly polite grin spread across his face as he waited for Madison to retell her very tall order. She stared into the case and tried to remember everything that she had just asked for.

She cleared her throat and donned the worst fake Canadian-who-summers-in-New-Jersey accent. Madison carefully assessed the dessert cases. "Right. Two of those, and four of these? Let's do three rice treats. Don't forget the slices of chocolate cake in the other case. We'll take two. We'll also have two coffees and maybe one of the coffee cakes."

Madison turned to Angie and asked, "Did I miss anything?"

Angie shook her head no as her eyes widened at Madison's impressive memory. Apparently, she functioned well under pressure.

Art scrambled to write down Madison's lengthy order. Casually, Madison sidled over to the counter. She tried to mimic Vincent's masculine gait as she closed the distance. Even from a distance, Madison recognized Art's handwriting. The handwritten warning was permanently stamped into her brain. She could recognize that handwriting anywhere. It just so happened to be right in front of her at this very moment.

Madison pressed against the front of the glass and looked straight at Art's handwriting. Art looked up at the intrusion and huffed, "Do you mind?"

"Not at all."

She stepped back and waited for Art to collect the order. He grabbed a large paper box and tossed the smaller pastries inside. He took his time and put the chocolate cake slices on top of the heap.

While Madison wasn't anywhere near a pro, the organizational choices distinctly reminded her of a misguided game of stacking blocks.

Art rang up the lengthy order. Angie reached into her wallet and pulled out her credit card. Alarm bells rang in the back of Madison's head as she quickly stepped forward and joked, "It's on me, friend. I insist."

She pulled out a wad of cash and handed it over to Art. Angie subtly arched a brow in Madison's direction. The two stared at each other until a look of understanding dawned across Angie's features. Her credit card would ruin their entire undercover scheme.

Art pushed the order across the counter and Madison nodded her thanks. She watched in horror as the corner of Angie's beard slipped down her face. It was time to go.

"Actually, hold this."

Madison handed the order over to Angie. Angie pressed the box against her mouth and drawled, "Woo. Smells darn delicious."

They were halfway to the door when Art shouted, "Wait!"

Chapter 34

Trepidation gripped the inside of Madison's stomach as she slowly turned back around. They were caught. The outfits were bad but their accents were terrible.

Madison waited to hear what tipped him off. Instead, Art held up two cups and called, "You forgot the coffee."

"Thanks."

Art held out the drinks and Madison swiftly grabbed them and moved away. Relief swept through her body as she prepared to exit the shop.

"Wait just a minute!"

Madison turned around, half expecting Art to be holding a few extra napkins. Instead, red-tinted his cheeks as he shoved a finger in Angie's direction and yelled, "Whatever you're doing, get out. You can't prove anything!"

He'd spotted the wayward mustache at the very last second. It didn't matter, Madison knew that they'd collected enough evidence to at least spark a tentative investigation.

"Go!"

The two fled the store and sped across the street to their blue stakeout rental car. Madison swung open the driver's door as Angie settled into the passenger's seat. Lenny sat in the middle of the backseat with a half-finished packet of red licorice on one side and an opened laptop on the other.

He looked over at the two haggard women and announced, "Nothing recorded."

Chapter 35

"I still think it was my best joke ever," Lenny chuckled as they sent the final piece of the story to their boss.

Angie shook her head, "No way. I almost had a heart attack. Do you know what a fake Canadian who summers in New Jersey sounds like?

Lenny frowned, "No, why?"

"Well, I do because that's the accent Madison used to disguise her voice."

Lenny burst out into full-blown belly laughs as they prepared to part ways. Given the amount of excitement that happened during the afternoon, they were making great time. Lenny and Angie would be right on schedule to grab their kids from school.

"See you ladies after Christmas."

"Merry Christmas, Lenny."

Angie and Madison waved goodbye as Lenny walked across the news station's parking lot. He drove away and his car's tires kicked up a spray of muddied water. The earlier snowfall had already melted into the ground.

"Do you think the evidence is enough to at least make the health inspectors reconsider?"

Madison stared off into the distance as she thought over everything that happened in the last few days. She hadn't spoken to Vincent since their squabble. Sure, Madison had sent him a quick text to keep him informed about the restaurant caper but that didn't really count as talking. After finding out what it felt like to settle into a nightly routine with someone else, her cozy cabin felt oddly lonely. Making cookies and coffee for one just wasn't the same. Madison hoped that she'd be able to help Vincent keep his restaurant. Madison knew she wouldn't be able to let the investigation go. A part of her hoped Vincent would be able to understand.

Angie balked, "Enough to reconsider! Are you kidding? This blows everything out of the water. I'm pretty sure you just saved most of the restaurants in town. My friend in the police station said they already arrested Art on suspicion of burglary."

"That's good."

Sensing Madison's muted excitement, Angie nudged, "What's wrong?"

If the situation wasn't so serious, Madison would have laughed. Angie's glued mustache clung on for dear life as half of it blew in the slight breeze. Instead of laughing, Madison offered a small smile.

She sighed, "I'm proud that we caught Art, but I still feel bad about all of the restaurants."

"Don't worry, things will get better. Besides, Lenny already sent the evidence to the police department. Looks like Lakewood will be back to normal just in time for Christmas."

"How do you know?"

"Lakewood has a way of taking care of its own. We'll make sure everyone gets back on their feet."

Madison nodded. With Christmas closing in, she needed to start getting ready for her recently added morning shift.

"That's good."

Angie nudged her side, "That also includes Vincent. Lenny added the footage from DeLuca's Restaurant, the attempted voting manipulation at the Christmas Festival, and the break-in at your house. And well, pretty much everything weird that's happened in Lakewood since that new bakery opened."

"You're right," Madison's short answers told a lengthy story of their own.

Bright dark orbs narrowed on Madison's features. Angie pressed, "What happened with Vincent?"

Madison rubbed a hand across her heavily-painted brow. "Honestly, I think it was a massive miscommunication. I was too eager to prove myself and couldn't see things from his perspective. I'll need to talk to him once everything settles down."

Angie sagely nodded and steered the conversation back to the soon-to-be best piece of investigative reporting that Lakewood had ever seen.

After a beat, Angie added, "I also included the ladder."

Madison rolled her eyes, "Who could forget the ladder?"

"Not us," Angie's eyes softened, "Look, thank you for taking my Christmas shift. It means a lot."

Madison hugged Angie. The restaurants were finally safe from more harm. The news channel had already contacted the authorities with proof of the crimes and soon an entire segment would run detailing Art's nefarious escapades around town. Jannie said that the network would air the segment before the new year. In the meantime, justice was already in the works.

"I'll text you my schedule for Christmas. Thank you."

“Don’t worry about it. Besides, what’s a good friendship worth?”

Angie laughed, “Everything.”

Chapter 36

For some reason, it wasn't the Christmas morning Madison had envisioned. She'd called her parents before work and thanked them for the nicely wrapped book. She'd been looking everywhere for the latest book from Makenna Lovejoy's mystery series.

She'd hustled off to work and was glad to arrive a little earlier than normal. Lenny had the day off so an eager intern stood in his place. For an entire hour, the intern talked about how much he enjoyed Christmas even though he didn't celebrate. Madison half-heartedly listened along as she prepared for the broadcast.

"Are you ready to start?"

A round eager face appeared near Madison's side. She looked at her watch and nodded her head. Her earpiece crackled as she got into position. Luckily, it was her first and only story for the day.

"I'm Madison Crawford and thank you for tuning into Channel 40 News. Merry Christmas."

The animal shelter positioned in the background proudly displayed an empty sign. All of the animals within Waverly's animal shelter were adopted for the holiday season. Madison grinned as she happily detailed the story. She highlighted the importance of committing to a pet for life. Madison held up several pictures of some recently adopted pets and their new owners. Madison finalized her broadcast and lowered her microphone.

The camera turned off and Madison gave the intern a high-five. He did a great job.

Maybe he'd stick around and act as Lenny's apprentice.

Madison checked her phone and noticed a vague text message from her boss. She didn't know what to make of it. Why would Jannie tell her to call right after a live broadcast? Hadn't she effortlessly executed the story?

Madison sighed and called her boss's cell. An energetic voice answered the phone in less than two rings.

"Guess what?"

"If it's bad news then don't tell me," Madison joked.

Her boss's surprisingly jovial voice rang through the phone. She replied, "The network loves your investigative flair. They'd love to see what else you can do."

Madison almost dropped the phone. The opportunity she'd always dreamed of was finally right in front of her. Unwilling to take all of the credit, Madison quickly added, "Lenny and Angie made it possible."

Her boss continued, "We spoke with them yesterday and they kept singing your praises. They said the story was your idea. Putting together an investigative piece takes vision and commitment. How would you feel about coming in next week to talk about your own local news segment?"

Madison swallowed as her throat tightened with excitement. She laughed, "Yes, I'd love to hear more."

"Perfect. Madison, you've really shown off your level of talent in the last few weeks and we're excited to see more."

"Thanks, Jannie"

"Merry Christmas."

She hung up her phone and watched the intern load the last of the equipment into the van. Technically, she was finished for the day. Madison thought over her plans. She could always try a new recipe from one of Mrs. Fullbright's recently gifted books. Of course, none of the books included Diane's festival famous cookie recipe.

"Need a ride?"

A masculine voice called from a few feet away. Vincent held a freshly baked apple pie. His lopsided grin disarmed Madison as he closed the distance.

"How did you find me?"

Vincent winced, "Angie told me you were taking her shift. I turned on the news and drove right over."

Madison looked over to the intern as he waited in the news van. She waved at her young coworker and explained, "You go ahead. Enjoy the rest of your day."

The intern grinned as he turned on the ignition and carefully turned out of the parking lot. Madison watched as the news van sped out of sight.

Vincent cleared his throat, "I'm sorry. I really put my foot in my mouth. I told you to let it go because I was too proud to admit that I was scared. I didn't want to say that the idea of you getting hurt keeps me up at night. I didn't want you to be in danger because of what was happening to the restaurant. I don't want you to be in danger, ever."

Madison disagreed, "Look, you were right to be concerned. I was being pretty risky."

"Yes, but that's part of your job and you were taking reasonable risks. Having Mrs.

Fullbright and Denise in the back of the bookstore when you confronted Art was a smart move."

"I wasn't open about what I was doing. I didn't want to lie to you, but I also didn't want you to worry."

Vincent nodded, "Angie explained what happened. Denise also has a way of painting a very colorful picture."

The duo laughed. A loud rumble jumped into the conversation and Madison blushed. She'd been in such a rush to arrive early for work that breakfast had fallen to the wayside.

"Can I interest you in an apology apple pie?"

"Is it one of your specialties?"

"No, but I'm learning. I can make a pretty amazing apple pie whenever the situation demands one."

"Let's give it a try."

Vincent handed Madison a spoon as they walked over to the pickup bed of his truck. The two clamored inside the pickup bed layered with pillows and a checkered blanket.

"You definitely know how to make an apology."

"Only because I'm trying to put aside my pride. Words and actions need to match."

"How's the restaurant?"

Vincent grinned, "You saved it. The health department is reconsidering the fines and the city is creating a program designed to help the impacted restaurants get back on their feet."

"That's amazing."

"You're amazing, Madison. You made this happen. Thank you."

His playful wink made Madison's heart flutter as they sat together and prepared to tuck into a delicious apple pie. A speck of white flitted from the sky and landed on one of the blanket's red boxes.

Madison narrowed her eyes. What an odd time for pollen. She shrugged and scooped her first bite of pie onto her spoon. She closed her eyes and savored the bite. The pie crust was baked to perfection with delicious morsels of spiced apple.

Okay, apology accepted.

"Madison," Vincent's voice purred in a timbre barely above a whisper.

"Yes?"

She looked up and met Vincent's gentle stare. He pointed up with his clean spoon. Madison followed his gesture with her gaze.

Snowflakes moved in gentle waves across the sky and landed in the surrounding trees. The first Christmas snow in over 100 years.

Madison sucked in a breath as she reached over the pie and squeezed Vincent's hand.

He grinned, "See, miracles do happen."

The End

Thank you for reading
Broadcasting Christmas Cheer:

Thank you for reading another novel within the wonderful Cozy Christmas series! I massively appreciate that you took the time to read my book. As a small indie author, every review helps.

I love hearing from readers while building a mystery-focused community. Thank you for reading small and thinking big!

Review Link:

http://amazon.com/review/create-review?&asin=B0CNYGHRO8

Mysteriously Delicious Recipe Index

FESTIVAL FAMOUS OOEY GOOEY CHRISTMAS COOKIES

4 Sticks of unsalted butter

4 Eggs

1 3/4 Cups brown sugar

1 1/2 Cups brown sugar

2 Teaspoons salt

2 Teaspoons baking soda

2 Teaspoons vanilla

4 1/4 Cups flour

4 1/2 Cups semi-sweet chocolate chips

2 1/2 Cups white chocolate chips

2 1/2 Cups dark chocolate chips

1 1/2 Cups butterscotch chips

Sprinkle sea salt

Bake at 375 degrees and keep checking after 8 minutes

CAMILLE CABRERA'S BOOKS:

Catalina's Tide
The Rule of Three
The Mystery of Mistletoe Motel
Chronometer
Our Perfect Murder
Lady Cavendish's Christmas Caper
Below the Water
The First Paper Cut: An Anniversary to Die For
Troublesome Trades: The Inkblot Crow Mystery
Troublesome Trades: Discovering the Glass Queen
Troublesome Trades: The Glass Slipper
Troublesome Trades: Crime Always Pays
Troublesome Trades: Feathers and Fate
Delivered
Broadcasting Christmas Cheer
A Very Coastal Christmas
Below Boston

CAMILLE CABRERA

Camille Cabrera is a #1 bestselling American mystery author. She specializes in sub genres such as noir and suspense. Her works often involve complicated and controversial female protagonists. She takes great pride creating works that revolve around a specific holiday to contrast the familiar celebration with the unknown shroud of death.

Cabrera's first Christmas mystery, THE MYSTERY OF MISTLETOE MOTEL, previously reached the number one spot on Amazon's Mystery Romance chart. LADY CAVENDISH'S CHRISTMAS CAPER ranked within the top 10 on four different Amazon charts during its debut month.

THE MYSTERY OF MISTLETOE MOTEL

Promising accountant Lacy Pondwater never wanted to own the Mistletoe Motel. However, when Lacy's mother passes away and her dad grows too old to readjust roof tiles, she scrambles, with the help of her younger sister Stacy, to keep the family business afloat. On a constantly shrinking shoestring budget, Lacy's maxed out every credit card and is at the end of her rope.

After a few too many glasses of wine and paranormal crime shows, Lacy embellishes the description of the Mistletoe Motel online to include Victorian era haunts and the occasional ghost encounter.

A question slowly circles around the back of Lacy's mind. Did she inadvertently invite a haunting to Mistletoe Motel, or are her eager guests merely manifesting their own adventures? Of course, white lies always come back to bite, and when a ghost hunting television show asks to film, the sisters reluctantly agree. Only a Christmas miracle can save the motel from bankruptcy and Lacy from a life of fraud.

THE MYSTERY OF MISTLETOE MOTEL

CHAPTER 1 TEASER…

"Dang it!" The expletive rolled from my tongue as steam nearly poured from my ears. My temper was about to erupt. The only thing holding back my verbal eruption of epic proportions was the tiniest bit of patience that I'd haphazardly taped back together, just like every single pipe and banister inside of our crumbling motel.

Stacy was so busted. How many times had I told her to make sure the meat locker was closed? How many times had I politely opened and closed it in front of her doe-eyed stare in the hopes that at least one lightbulb would turn on in that willfully empty house
of a brain? Too many. Now, she was so dead. Well, more figuratively than literally. She was my younger sister, after all.

Of course, I knew that I wasn't being fair. Stacy had a great heart with a wonderfully vibrant open mind, but sometimes her attempts at helpfulness really made it
difficult to keep the motel afloat. Her real calling was instructing yoga classes in an outdoor setting surrounded by vibrant people and my real calling was
hiding behind piles of papers dotted with tiny numbers.

Unfortunately, both of our dreams were currently put on hold for the greater purpose of saving the legacy that our parents had left us. It felt like I'd mentally carved out a room in my mind for

accounting and simply got up and left the next day. I hadn't even
settled into the role for a full day before saving the family business rightly took priority. Maybe once everything has settled I could one day follow along as Stacy teaches a yoga class. Until then, we were stuck
working together with tensions beyond high and stress levels operating at maximum capacity.

We weren't always like this. I shook away the thoughts from another time and snapped back to the moment. A new fresh wave of anxiety masked as fear zipped through my bloodstream.

I could just picture Stacy's slim arms folded over her chest as her statuesque features turned shocked and tinged with embarrassment. I angrily stomped around
the piles of ruined meat products. The gene pool had played the opposite card with me. It had graciously provided me with all of the potential to be an excellent accountant as well as all of the love of pastries to also be in competition with the Pillsbury Doughboy. At least, that's how I felt living through
my early teens and rougher-than-needed middle school years in a small town. It was something that had really bothered me in my youth, but nearly a decade later, it now meant that I enjoyed my little dimples and curves in a way that younger me would
take ten years to fully understand.

The slight stench told me the meat was bad, but that didn't stop the dreamer in me from personally inspecting every single thawed rib-

eye by hand. The earliest risers in the motel were about to get up and the Mistletoe Motel had no viable meat options for our widely broadcasted continental breakfast. It
was a tradition from our parents that Stacy and I had yet to throw away. No matter how costly. Sentiments were expensive.

In all honesty, we only had a single room booked and that was still more than our usual occupancy rate. The real problem was that we no longer had any meat for ourselves or any future potential guests. A girl could
dream of the latter.

Worse still, we had no viable meat for breakfast, lunch, or dinner for the next week. That was a more realistic hurdle. I rubbed my face in agitation as my messy mop of brown hair remained barely restrained
by a threadbare hairband. I ran my tongue over my
slightly crooked bottom teeth and felt the worn grooves and ridges. I had planned to get them straightened after college, but that was no longer in the cards for now. The bottom teeth were pushed together like a hungry shark. The dentist had said that
the enamel would likely slowly erode if left untreated. I had laughed until tears had threatened to fall at the literal metaphor for the state of the motel that now resided on the inside of my mouth. It was a visible fixer-upper and a ticking time bomb of repercussions that was just waiting to explode.

Not that I minded. Well, maybe I did care and that's why this meat-locker-gate was just the perfect excuse to release some steam.

Two flights of well-worn cream carpeted stairs later and I huffed, hunched over, directly outside of Stacy's room. My long fingers rapped against the wooden door as I called, "Stacy, get up, you murderer! The meat locker was left open and everything inside has gone bad. I need to go shopping
for food. Please watch the front desk!"

Lady Cavendish's Christmas Caper
CHAPTER 1 TEASER...

Flames hungrily licked around the burnt edges as angry dark spots marred the once pristine surface. Charlie instinctively knew all was lost. She had ruined the triple-layer bean casserole.

Clouds of smoke swirled around the kitchen as Charlie opened the ancient windows of her rustic Montana cabin. A fresh breeze rolled into the tiny abode and granted her a momentary reprieve from the smelly mess. She didn't have enough money to run out to the store and replace the charred dinner. It didn't help that the nearest store was nearly an hour away by car. The recipe had seemed simpler online.

Like usual, easier said than done.

Defeated, Charlie grumbled into the air "I guess a microwave dinner will do."

She cleaned up the kitchen and triple-checked that the small blaze had gone out. The remnants of the casserole resembled congealed plastic. She poured a cup of water onto the mess, just to be safe. With Charlie's luck, anything was possible. It wasn't exactly like she was living the high life, running between her job at the sports bar and her part-time gig at the mall. She was exhausted and too strapped for cash to spring for a pizza. She wondered what it would feel like to have enough loose pocket change to buy a pizza after an unfortunate kitchen accident. The prospect of a few extra dollars felt as foreign as an international vacation.

A commotion near the front door suddenly commanded Charlie's attention. She grabbed the nearest item within reach and held it up. The wooden serving spoon did little to boost Charlie's confidence as she crept closer to the locked door. An odd thick packet had landed on her wooden floor. The mail slot's cover swung back and forth from the force of the recent gift. Charlie looked down and noticed a bright red stamp that indicated a priority delivery. The parcel already commanded Charlie's full attention. She did not work in a field or live in an environment that called for any remotely time-sensitive deliveries.

Her curiosity got the best of her. She reached down and inspected the item. Charlie noticed the foreign postage and assumed it was a gift from her loving, mischievous grandmother. The two hadn't spoken in a little over a month. Wi-Fi was spotty living near the Rocky Mountains. The intense rainstorms only added to the typically temperamental connection.

A pile of assumptions jostled around in the back of Charlie's mind. Maybe her grandma had finally received her belated Christmas gift. Charlie knew that it wasn't her proudest moment. The gift was over a week late, but she tried.

Unconvinced the package belonged to her, Charlie double-checked the address. The package proudly stated it was intended for Charlotte Cavendish.

Charlie wrinkled her nose as she read her real name. Sure, Charlotte was a gorgeous name, but it just didn't fit. Charlottes were sophisticated and had plans. And Charlie, well, she was happy when she made a casserole without setting off the smoke detectors. She felt more like a Charlie. In her mind, a Charlie was still deciding where to go while a Charlotte was already driving full speed ahead.

Charlie slid her finger down the side of the thick envelope. She unfolded the sheets and read the first paragraph. Her mouth hung open in surprise. The letter was requesting her presence at the reading of Lady Cavendish's will.

Charlie itched her nose and wondered, "Who is Lady Cavendish?"

9 798330 557752